A Dear Little Girl at School

Amy Ella Blanchard

Copyright © 2023 Culturea Editions
Text and cover : © public domain
Edition : Culturea (Hérault, 34)
Contact : infos@culturea.fr
Print in Germany by Books on Demand
Design and layout : Derek Murphy
Layout : Reedsy (https://reedsy.com/)
ISBN : 9791041818471
Légal deposit : July 2023

A Dear Little Girl at School

CHAPTER I

COUSIN BEN

Edna and Cousin Ben Barker were on the back porch. It was a favorite place, for it was always shady there in summer and out of the wind on cold days. If big Cousin Ben did not always like to be where Edna was, on the other hand Edna invariably sought out Cousin Ben if he were to be found about the premises.

On this special afternoon he was doing something to his wheel, getting it in order for a long ride which he had planned for the next day. Edna stood watching him, ready to hand a tool or run for a piece of rag to be used in cleaning, or to fill the oil can from the bottle on the shelf upstairs.

"Where are you going to-day, Cousin Ben?" Edna always asked this for Cousin Ben's replies were generally so funny.

"I'm going to the woods," he said, "to see Johnny-jump-up."

"Why will he jump up?" asked Edna in pleased expectancy of something amusing.

"Because the dog-wood bark, you know."

"I know dog-wood blossoms," returned Edna a little doubtfully.

"Of course, and I dare say you know the dog-wood bark, too, don't you?"

"Ye-es, I suppose so."

Cousin Ben went on burnishing the metal he was at work upon. "You see," he continued after a moment, "the catkins will all be out and when I meet one I shall say, 'Pussy, will oh, will you tell me the way to the elder Berries.'"

"What do you suppose she will say?" inquired Edna settling herself well content to continue this sort of talk, though thinking it was scarcely the season for Pussy-willows.

"She will say: 'The elder Berry? My dear boy, any dog ought to know the way there.' You see she knows I am a Barker."

Edna laughed. "Go on."

"And I will say, 'Yes, madam, but that sassy Fras always tries to get in my path. It is a very easy matter to whip poor Will, but sassy Fras is another matter.' Then she will ask: 'Did you ever try to haze L. Nutt?' and I will reply, 'Chestnuts!' for I don't like to talk about hazing, being in a position to expect a little of it any day. Well, Ande, I must be off or I will find Pip's sis away." Cousin Ben always called Edna Ande because he declared that was what her name really was but had been turned hind side before. Some persons, Edna's sister Celia and Agnes Evans, for instance, called Cousin Ben a very silly boy, but Edna thought his kind of nonsense great fun.

It was an afternoon in autumn. For some time past, Edna and her sister had been going into the city to school every day, but this was the last week when this would be done, for after this they would go only on Mondays returning on Fridays till the days became long again. During the winter when it was still dark at seven in the morning, and when the afternoons were so short, it had seemed better that they should not come home every day. Therefore, as Aunt Elizabeth Horner and Uncle Justus wanted much to have them remain, it was so arranged. Edna was a great favorite with her Uncle Justus, for she had spent the winter previous at his house and had gone to his school. Then, on account of Mr. Conway's business, the family had removed from the town in which they had formerly lived and had taken a house a little out of the city.

Like most children Edna loved the country and was glad of the change. A little further up the road lived her friend Dorothy Evans and her sister Agnes, the latter was a little older than Edna's sister Celia. All four girls attended Uncle Justus' school and so did Margaret MacDonald, the adopted daughter of good Mrs. MacDonald who lived in the big gray stone house with the lovely grounds. Margaret was having a pretty hard time of it, as she had never had much opportunity of going to school and was far behind the girls of her own age. Edna and Dorothy were her staunch defenders, however and when matters came to a too difficult pass the older girls were appealed to and could always straighten out whatever was wrong. Frank and Charlie, Edna's brothers, were almost too large for Uncle Justus' school, where only little fellows went, so they went elsewhere to the school which Roger and Steve Porter attended. It was Cousin Ben's first year at college, and he was housed at the Conways, his mother being an elder sister of Edna's mother.

After seeing Cousin Ben start off, Edna left the porch and stood for a moment thinking what she would do next. This being the last time she would be at home for the entire week, she concluded she ought to make the most of it, but first she must get together such things as she should want for Monday. "Tuesday, Wednesday and Thursday afternoons, and Monday, too. There are only four, after all," she said, counting the days on her fingers. "It seems very much longer when you first think of it." And then, as she continued to think, to her surprise she discovered that only Tuesdays, Wednesdays and Thursdays would be the entire days she would spend away from home.

She was so interested in having found this out that she ran upstairs to her mother, to tell of it. "Mother," she said, "I have made a discovery."

"You have, and what is it?" said Mrs. Conway.

"Why, here I've been thinking I'd be away from you the whole week all but Saturday and Sunday, and now I find out I shall see you every day but three, 'cause, you know, I don't start till after breakfast on Monday, so that's one day. Then Tuesday, Wednesday and Thursday I don't see you, but I get back in time for dinner on Friday, so there is Friday, Saturday and Sunday, three more days. Isn't it fine?"

"Very, I think."

"And the funny part is," Edna went on busily thinking, "I am at school five days out of the seven. It's almost like a puzzle, isn't it? I think I shall take Ada with me and leave her there. She is used to it, and won't mind as much as some of the other dolls, for she was there all last year and besides, Aunt Elizabeth gave her to me. Aunt Elizabeth is quite kind sometimes, isn't she?"

"She means to be kind all the time, but she has rather a stern manner."

"Did you used to be afraid of her when you were a little girl?"

"No, honey, because I didn't know her. She is your papa's aunt, you know."

"And he told me he didn't see much of her, for he lived in quite another place, and I suppose by the time he grew up he wasn't afraid of anybody. Well, anyhow, I'm glad it won't be 'butter or molasses' all the week."

"What do you mean, dearie?"

"Why, you know we couldn't have both and there were never any preserves. Sometimes there were stewed apples, the dried kind, and they were not so very bad when they were sweet enough and had a lot of lemon flavor in them. I used to ask Ellen to do them that way and she always would, except when Aunt Elizabeth was in the kitchen and then she had to do as Aunt Elizabeth told her. If you have more preserves than you can use, don't you think you could send her some, mother? You see we shall not be here to eat them, Celia and I, and you won't have to use so many."

"That is an idea. Why, yes, I can send some in every week when you go, and Celia can tell Aunt Elizabeth to have them for your supper."

"How will she tell her?" asked Edna, feeling that this was an ordeal that she would not like to go through.

5

"Why, it will be very easy to say, 'Aunt Elizabeth, here are some preserves mother thought would be nice for supper to-night.' Don't you think that would be easy to say?"

"Ye-es," returned Edna a little doubtful if this would have the proper effect. "I think myself it would be better to let Ellen have them or Uncle Justus."

Her mother laughed. Edna's awe of Aunt Elizabeth was so very apparent.

"There is one thing I wish you would promise," the little girl went on, "and that is, that you will always have hot cakes on Saturday mornings so I can have butter and syrup both."

"I promise," replied her mother smiling.

"I know Louis is mighty glad not to be going back," Edna continued, "and I'm rather glad he isn't myself, for this year I shall have Celia."

"I thought you were fond of Louis."

"I am pretty fond of him, but I'd rather have girls about all the time than boys all the time. Girls fuss with you, of course. They get mad and won't speak, but I'd liefer they'd do that than try to boss you the way boys do. Mother, there is another thing I wish you would do, and that is I wish you would tell Aunt Elizabeth that she will please let Dorothy come to play with me sometimes. Dorothy is my particular friend, you know, and Aunt Elizabeth will never allow me to have her visit me unless you say she can."

"Did she never allow you to have company last winter?"

Edna shook her head and a sigh escaped her.

"I will arrange that Dorothy shall come," said her mother quite firmly.

"It's going to be much nicer than last year," remarked Edna in a satisfied tone, "for I shall always have Celia to go to, and you will be so near, too, and besides I like Uncle Justus much better than I did at first."

"Of the two I should think you would have more fear of Uncle Justus than of Aunt Elizabeth," said her mother looking down at her.

"I did at first, but I found it was mostly on account of his eyebrows; they are so shaggy."

Mrs. Conway smiled. "I have heard it said that he can be rather terrible," she remarked.

"Oh, well, so he can, but he isn't all the time and Aunt Elizabeth is."

"I hope this year you will find out that it is only Aunt Elizabeth's eyebrows, too."

"It couldn't be, for she hasn't any to speak of," returned Edna. As she talked she was carefully packing the little trunk in which Ada's clothes were kept. It was a tiny trunk, only about six inches long. Aunt Elizabeth had made it, herself, by covering a box with leather and strapping the leather across with strips of wood glued on. Edna liked the trunk much better than a larger one which had been bought at the store. Aunt Elizabeth was very clever in making things of this kind and would sometimes surprise her little niece with some home-made gift which was the more prized because it was unusual. The child remembered this now and began to feel that she had not shown herself very grateful in speaking as she had done a moment before. "Mother," she said. "I didn't mean that Aunt Elizabeth was frightful all the time. She is very kind when she gives me things like this trunk."

"You don't mean frightful," replied Mrs. Conway laughing, "you mean she is rather formidable."

But that was too much of a word for Edna, though she did not say so. Having stowed away Ada's belongings, three frocks, two petticoats, a red hood and sacque, a blue dressing-gown and apron, she shut the lid. "I don't think I'll take her furs this week because she'll not need them," she remarked, "and I don't think I will take any of my other dolls because I will be so glad to see them next Friday. Mother, if you come into town any time during the week will you come out to see us?"

"If I have time I certainly shall."

Edna gave a sigh of content. It was surely going to be much better than last year. "Mother," she said, changing the subject, "do you think Cousin Ben is silly?"

"He can be rather silly but he can also be very sensible. He is silly only when he wants to tease or when he wants to amuse a little girl I know."

"I like his silly better than some of the big girls's sillies. They giggle so much and aren't funny at all. I think he is very funny. He says such queer things about the trees and plants in the woods. He twists their names around so they mean something else. Like the dog-wood, bark, you know. Mother, what is hazing?"

"It is the kind of thing the college boys do to those in a lower class; they play tricks on them which sometimes are really very cruel."

"Do you mean they really hurt them?"

"Sometimes they hurt them very much. I knew of one young man who was forced into a pond of water on an icy day in the fall, and who nearly died of pneumonia in consequence of the cold he took from having to be in his wet clothes so long."

"Do you think they will do anything like that to Cousin Ben?"

"I certainly hope not, though no doubt there will be some tricks played on him as he is a Freshman."

Edna knew what a Freshman was but the matter of hazing was quite new to her and troubled her very much. Cousin Ben had gone out alone to the woods. Perhaps this very moment someone was lying in wait for him.

Hastily setting away the doll and trunk she ran downstairs, put on her coat and hat and started up the road toward the woods nearest. She had no exact plan in her mind, but she knew Cousin Ben had probably gone to see one of his classmates who lived just beyond this piece of woods. The college was on the outskirts of the city and the dormitories were within easy walking distance, so that one was liable to see a group of college boys at almost any time. Edna trotted along hoping to overtake her cousin. She did not believe anyone would attack him unless he were alone, and she meant to keep him company on his return walk. Just as she reached the edge of the woods she came upon a group of Sophomores standing a short distance away and she heard one say. "We'll nab him as he comes out, boys."

Who could they mean but Cousin Ben? She walked slowly that she might, if possible, hear more.

"You're sure he came this way?" she heard another say.

"Sure," was the reply. "We saw him go in Abercrombie's gate."

That settled it in Edna's mind, for it was Will Abercrombie whose house Cousin Ben most frequented. She hesitated a moment, wondering what path her cousin would take, and then she remembered that the short cut was through the woods; it was much longer by the road. It was already getting rather late and it looked grim and gloomy in the woods, but there was nothing to do but face any danger and go straight ahead. She was crafty enough not to turn in at once for fear the boys might suspect, so she kept on a short distance to where the road turned and then she cut into the bit of forest scrambling up the bank and scratching her hands, with the brambles, but reaching the path in a few minutes. The further she went the darker it grew. The sun was setting and she could see long fingers of light between the trees. She wished she had some one with her, that Cousin Ben would appear before she went much further, but there was no sign of him and she plodded on, the dead leaves rustling about her feet or falling from overhead, giving her little starts of fear. It seemed a long, long way, and she almost wished she had not undertaken the work of rescue, but at last she saw, dimly ahead of her, a figure approaching and heard a cheerful whistling which she recognized as her cousin's. And she darted forward to meet him.

CHAPTER II

THE SECRET

Cousin Ben striding along did not at first see the little girl, but at her calling "Cousin Ben, Cousin Ben," he stopped short.

"Why, you little monkey, what are you doing here?" he said. "The bugaboos will catch you here in these dark woods."

"There isn't such a thing as bugaboos," returned Edna stoutly, "and I should be very silly to think so, but something will catch you if you don't look out."

"'The gob-e-lins will get you if you don't look out,'" replied Cousin Ben, laughing. "Is that what you are trying to say? If you are not afraid of bugaboos neither am I afraid of goblins. What do you think is going to get a big fellow like me?"

"Why," said Edna at once becoming serious, "I will tell you; I heard some college boys talking back there by the edge of the woods."

"You did? and what did they say?"

"They said: 'We'll nab him as he comes out, boys.'"

"Humph! What did they look like? Did you know any of them?"

"The one who said that was John Fielding, and there was another that I've seen before. He sits back of our pew at church."

"Sophs, both of them, and did you come all this way to tell me about it?"

"Why, yes, I was afraid they wanted to haze you."

"What do you know about hazing?"

"Mother told me about a young man who nearly died of pneumonia because some of the boys doused him in cold water, in a pond or something."

"And you didn't want me to have pneumonia. I won't on this occasion, I promise you. I think we can circumnavigate those fellows. I won't see Johnny-jump-up to-day."

Edna laughed. "Won't they be disappointed?"

"They will that. Now come along and let's get out of here."

"Which way shall we go?"

"Oh, we will take the back road and come out there below the MacDonald barn so they won't get a hint of our coming home, for the barn is below the woods, you know. It is a little further, but I hope you don't mind that."

"No, indeed, I am so glad to have you get out of the way of those boys."

"If I can manage to side-track them for a while perhaps they won't be so keen. I thought they had it in for me, and have been rather expecting an onslaught."

They cut through the woods, coming out the other side and taking a short road not much used, which brought them out a little distance from the main road which was then easily reached. "Now we're safe," said Edna with satisfaction as she saw her own gate.

"We? You don't suppose they'd haze you, do you?"

"Oh, no, but I feel safer when I am near home."

Ben dropped his bantering tone when they came up to the gate. "I say, Edna," he said, "you are a real Trojan to do this for me, and I shall not forget it in a hurry. Lots of big girls and boys, too, would have let the thing go, and not have taken the trouble. I am a thousand times obliged to you."

"Oh, but I wanted to do it, you know. I should have been very unhappy if anything had happened to you."

"I believe you would," returned Ben seriously; and they went in the house together.

This was the last Edna heard of hazing and if Cousin Ben was ever caught he did not tell her or anyone else.

Monday came around quite soon enough and Edna started off with her sister Celia to go to the city. It seemed quite natural to be back in the room which she had occupied the year before, only now Celia would share it with her. Ada was put in her old place on a little chair, her trunk by her side, and then the two girls went down to the school-room where a number of the pupils had already gathered. One of these was Clara Adams, a little girl whom Edna was sorry to see entering the school that year. She was a spoiled, discontented child who was continually pouting over some fancied grievance, and was what Dorothy and Edna called "fusty." For some reason she was always trying to pick a quarrel with Edna, and by the whispering which went on when Edna entered the room and the sidelong looks which were cast at her, as two or three girls, with hands to mouths, nudged one another, she felt sure that on this special occasion she was being talked about. However, she paid no attention to this little group but went over to where Dorothy was sitting and began to tell her about the preserves which Celia had successfully given in Ellen's charge.

At recess the same group of girls which had been whispering in the morning, again gathered in one corner and began their talk in low tones. Clara Adams was in the centre and it was she to whom the others were all looking. Clara was a favorite because of her wealth rather than because of her disposition, and she had followers who liked to have it said that they were intimate with her.

"What do you suppose they are talking about?" said Dorothy after a while.

"I'm sure I don't know and what's more I don't care," replied Edna. "Do you care, Dorothy?"

"Oh, I don't know; just a little, I think. See, they are going over and whispering to Molly Clark, and she is getting up and going over there. I wonder what it is all about."

Edna wondered, too, but neither she nor Dorothy found out that day. The same thing went on the next day. One by one most of the girls whom Edna and Dorothy liked the best were seen to join the little company of whisperers, and whenever Clara Adams would pass the two friends she would give them a look as much as to say: Wouldn't you like to know what we know?

"I think it is just horrid mean of them," said Dorothy when the next day came and they were no nearer to knowing the secret than they had been in the beginning.

"I heard Molly say something about to-morrow afternoon," said Edna. "They are all going to do something or go somewhere. I am going to tell sister, so I am."

"And I'll tell my sister. Maybe they know something about it, Edna."

They lost no time in seeking out their sisters to whom they made known the state of affairs. "And they are getting hold of nearly all the nicest girls," complained Edna. "Molly Clark, and Ruth Cutting and all those. They haven't said anything to Margaret, for I asked her. She isn't here to-day."

"Have you any idea what they are going to do?" Dorothy asked her sister.

"I have an idea, but it may not be right."

"Oh, tell us, do." The two younger girls were very eager.

12

Agnes leaned over and said in a low voice, "I believe they are getting up some sort of club."

"Oh!" This idea had never occurred to either of the little girls before.

"And they don't want us in it," said Edna, "I wonder why."

"It is all that horrid Clara Adams," declared Dorothy. "She is jealous of you because you always know your lessons and behave yourself, and she don't like me because I go with you and won't give you up for her."

"How do you know?" asked Edna.

"I know," returned Dorothy, and then she shut her lips very tightly.

"All the girls used to like us," said Edna sadly.

"Bless your dear heart," said Agnes drawing the child to her, "I shouldn't care. They will be sorry enough after a while, you may be sure, and will wish they had treated you two better. Celia, we mustn't let those little whippersnappers have it all their own way. Never you mind, children, we'll do something, too. Celia and I will talk it over and let you know to-morrow. You and Celia come up to our house Saturday afternoon and we'll see if we can get Margaret and perhaps one or two others. Now run along and let us talk over a plan I have."

The two went off joyously, arms around one another. When Agnes championed their cause there was no more reason to be troubled, and they finished their recess in a corner by themselves quite content.

There were not more than a dozen little girls in the class and when half of these had gone over to the enemy, and one or two were absent it left a very small number for Edna and Dorothy to count upon, but they did not care after the older girls had taken up their cause, and they cast quite as independent looks at Clara as she did at them. They would have a secret too. "And it will be a great deal nicer than theirs," declared Dorothy. So when the bell rang they went back to their seats in a very happy frame of mind.

The next day a new pupil appeared and at recess she was swooped down upon by one of Clara's friends and was borne away, but after a while she left the group and went back to her seat. Dorothy and Edna were out in the school yard playing, but when they came in the new scholar looked smilingly at Edna and after a while she made her way to where they were standing. "Isn't this Edna Conway?" she asked.

"Yes, I'm Edna," was the reply from the little round-faced girl who smiled at her.

"I'm Jennie Ramsey, and my mother told me to be sure to speak to you and tell you I was at the fair last year and I was so glad when you got the doll."

"Oh, were you there?" Edna looked pleased. "I am so glad you have come here to school. This is Dorothy Evans."

Jennie and Dorothy smiled at each other and Edna went on. "Dorothy don't you remember about Mrs. Ramsey who took so much trouble to get Margaret away from that dreadful woman? She must be a lovely mother, for she was so dear to Margaret."

"Do tell me about her," said Jennie. "I have been so much interested, for mother told me all about how you ran against her in the street and how you won the doll for her and all about her being adopted so I did hope I should know you some day. I'd like to be friends, if you will let me."

"Oh, I'd love to be," Edna spoke heartily, "and I am so glad you know about Margaret. She comes here to school, but of course she isn't very happy about having to be in the class with such little girls. Mrs. MacDonald is talking of getting a governess for her till she can catch up a little, but we shall be sorry to have her not come here."

"Do you know Clara Adams?" Dorothy asked. "I mean did you know her before you came to school?"

"Yes, I know her. She is in my Sunday-school class," returned Jennie, but she said nothing more, yet both the other two felt quite sure that there was no likelihood of Jennie's going over to the other faction. Then the bell rang and they all took their seats.

"Don't you like her?" whispered Edna before Miss Ashurst had taken her place.

Dorothy nodded yes, and glanced across at Clara who curled her lip scornfully.

When school was dismissed Jennie and Dorothy walked home together. Agnes and Dorothy remained in the city during the week just as the two Conway sisters had begun to do. Edna sought her sister Celia after dinner when the two had their study hour. "Isn't it nice," said Edna, "Jennie Ramsey has come to school, and she is such a nice little girl. I heard Uncle Justus say once that Mrs. Ramsey was much wealthier than Mrs. Adams but that one never saw her making any pretence because of her money. What is pretence, sister?"

"It is pretending, I suppose. I think he meant she didn't put on airs because of having money."

14

Edna nodded. She quite understood. "Wasn't it lovely for Jennie to want to be friends? She said her mother told her to be sure to speak to me, and, oh, sister, we saw one of the other girls go over and try to get her to join Clara's set and she didn't stay but came over to us. She said she knew Clara but I don't believe she likes her. Did you and Agnes talk about, you know what?"

"Yes, and we'll tell you but you mustn't ask me any questions now for I shall not answer. Now let us get to work or Aunt Elizabeth will be down on us for talking in study hour."

Edna turned her attention to her books and in a moment was not thinking of anything but her geography.

She could scarcely wait till the next day, however, when she and Dorothy should learn what Agnes had planned, but alas, she was not allowed this pleasure for Aunt Elizabeth called her from the school-room just at recess and took her down to see Miss Martin, the daughter of the rector of the church. Of course Edna was very glad to see Miss Martin, for she was very fond of her, but she did wish she had chosen some other day to call, and not only was Edna required to remain down in the parlor during the whole of recess but she was again summoned before she had a chance to speak a word to anyone at the close of school. This time it was to run an errand to the shop where an order had been forgotten and Edna was despatched to bring home the required article, Ellen being too busy to be spared.

She felt rather out of sorts at having both of her opportunities taken from her. "I don't see why they couldn't have sent sister," she said to herself, "or why they couldn't do without rice for just this once. I should think something else would be better, anyway, for dessert than rice and sugar." But there was no arranging Aunt Elizabeth's affairs for her and when the dish of rice appeared Edna was obliged to eat it in place of any other dessert. Her ill humor passed away, however, when Uncle Justus looked at her from under his shaggy brows and asked her if she didn't want to go to Captain Doane's with him. This was a place which always delighted her, for Captain Doane had been all over the world and had brought back with him all sorts of curiosities. Moreover, there was always a supply of preserved ginger taken from a queer jar with twisted handles, and there was also an especially toothsome cake which the captain's housekeeper served, so Edna felt that the feast in store for her, quite made up for the poverty of a dessert of boiled rice and sugar.

She wondered that Celia was not also asked to go, but she remembered that Celia did not know Captain Doane, and that probably she would think it very stupid to play with shells and other queer things while two old gentlemen talked on politics or some such dry subject. Therefore she went off very happily, rather glad that after all there was a pleasure for this day and one in prospect for the morrow.

15

CHAPTER III

A SATURDAY AFTERNOON

By Friday, Jennie, Dorothy and Edna had become quite intimate. Margaret was still kept at home by a bad cold, so these three little girls played at recess together joined by one or two others who had not been invited, or had not chosen, to belong to what the rest called "Clara Adams's set." There had been a most interesting talk with Agnes and Celia and a plan was proposed which was to be started on Saturday afternoon. Jennie had been invited to come, and was to go home with Dorothy after school to be sent for later.

Edna was full of the new scheme when she reached home on Friday, and she was no sooner in the house than she rushed up stairs to her mother. "Oh, mother," she cried, "I am so glad to see you, and I have so much to tell you."

"Then come right in and tell it," said her mother kissing her. "You don't look as if you had starved on bread and molasses."

Edna laughed. "Nor on rice. I hope you will never have rice on Saturdays, mother."

"Rice is a most wholesome and excellent dish," returned her mother. "See how the Chinese thrive on it. I am thinking it would be the very best thing I could give my family, for it is both nourishing and cheap. Suppose you go down and tell Maria to have a large dishful for supper instead of what I have ordered."

Edna knew her mother was teasing, so she cuddled up to her and asked: "What did you order, mother?"

"What should you say to waffles and chicken?"

"Oh, delicious!"

"But where is that great thing you were going to tell me?"

"Oh, I forgot. Well, when we got to school last Monday, there was Clara Adams and all the girls she could get together and they were whispering in a corner. They looked over at me and I knew they were talking about me, but I didn't care. Then I went over to Dorothy and we just stayed by ourselves all the time, for those other girls didn't seem to want to have anything to do with us. We hadn't done one single thing to make them act so, but Clara Adams is so hateful and jealous and all that, she couldn't bear to have us be liked by anybody. Dorothy told me she heard her say I was a pet and that was the reason I got along with my lessons. You know I study real hard, mother, and it

16

isn't that at all. Clara said it was just because Uncle Justus favored me, and told Miss Ashurst too. Wasn't that mean?"

"I think it was rather mean, but you must not mind what a spoiled child like Clara says, as long as you know it isn't so."

"That's what Agnes says. We told Agnes and Celia how the girls were doing and how they had a secret and didn't want us to be in it, so Agnes said we could have a secret, too, and she has planned a beautiful one, she and Celia. I will tell you about it presently. Well, then Jennie Ramsey came."

"Jennie Ramsey? I don't think I ever heard you speak of her."

"No, of course you didn't, for I only just became acquainted with her. Mother, don't you remember the lovely Mrs. Ramsey that did so much about getting Margaret into the Home of the Friendless?"

"I remember, now."

"Well, she is Jennie's mother, and she told Jennie to be sure to speak to me, because she knows Aunt Elizabeth, I suppose, but anyhow, she did. But first the Clara Adams set tried to get Jennie to go with them, but she just wouldn't, and so she's on our side. I know Clara is furious because the Ramseys are richer than the Adamses."

"Oh dear, oh dear," Mrs. Conway interrupted, "this doesn't sound a bit like my little girl talking about one person being richer than another and about one little girl's being furious about another's making friends with whom she chooses."

Edna was silent for a moment. "Mother," she said presently, "it is all Clara Adams's doings. If she wouldn't speak to us nor let the other girls play with us, why, what could we do?"

"I really don't know, my darling, we'll talk of that directly. Go on with your story."

"Well, so Agnes found out they were getting up a club and didn't want us in it, so she said we could have a club, too, and we're going to begin this afternoon—no, to-morrow afternoon. Mrs. Ramsey let Jennie go home with Dorothy to stay till to-morrow and she is going to send the automobile for her. She comes to school in the automobile every morning. I wish we had one then we wouldn't have to stay in town all the week."

"Dear blessed child, I am afraid Clara Adams is turning your head."

"Clara? why she doesn't even speak to me."

"All the same you are beginning to care more for the things that are important to her than ever you did before. Never mind, we'll talk about that later. Is that all?"

"It's about all, for we haven't had the club meeting yet. Agnes says she will start it and be the president for a month. Celia is going to be the secretary and when we know just what to do and how to carry it on then they will resign and some of us younger girls will be the officers."

Mrs. Conway smiled to hear all this grown-up talk, but she looked a little serious a moment after.

Edna watched her face. "Don't you approve of it, mamma," she asked anxiously.

"Of the club? Oh, yes, if it is the right kind of one. I will ask Celia about it, but what I don't like is that you should start it in a spirit of trying to get the better of another girl, though I can see that it is the most natural thing in the world for you to feel as you do, and I can see that Clara has really brought it on herself, but I do want my dear little girls to be charitable and above the petty meanness that is actuating Clara."

"Then what do you think we ought to do?"

"I am not sure. I shall have to think it over. In the meantime by all means start your club. Where is Celia?"

"She went out with the boys to look at the new pigeons, but I wanted to see you first."

Edna enjoyed the prospect of chicken and waffles too much to long too ardently for the next day. She hadn't seen Cousin Ben yet so she went out to hunt him up, but discovering that he was hard at work over his studies she concluded not to disturb him but to go with the boys to hear them expatiate upon the qualities of the new pigeons, of the trade they had made with another boy and of various things which had been going on at their school.

Great preparations were made for the first meeting of the club. In the Evans house was a large attic, one corner of which Agnes and Celia turned into a club-room. The house was an old-fashioned one, and the attic window was small. There was, too, an odor of camphor and of soap, a quantity of the latter being stored up there, but these things did not in the least detract from the place in the eyes of the girls. What they wanted was mystery, a place which was out of the way, and one specially set aside for their meetings. A small table was dragged out of the recesses of the attic. It was rather wobbly, but a bit of wood was put under the faulty leg, and it did very well. One perfectly good chair was brought up for the president, the rest were content to be seated on whatever came handy, two chairs very much gone as to backs, one with the bottom entirely through, and a rickety camp stool made up the remainder of the furniture, but Agnes had taken care that there were flowers on the table and that pens, pencils and paper were supplied. She also brought up some books "to make it look more literary," she said, and the organizers of the club were delighted.

They came whispering and with suppressed giggles up the steep stairway, made their way between piles of trunks and boxes to where Agnes sat in state, a call-bell before her. Margaret, much bundled up, had been permitted to join them, so they were the respectable number of six.

That morning the president and secretary had been closeted for an hour with Mrs. Conway and whatever they had determined upon in the beginning which seemed in the least unworthy was smitten from the plan.

The girls disposed themselves upon the various seats, Celia taking a place at the end of the table provided for the officers. There was much stifling of laughter and suppressed whispers before Agnes tapped the bell and said in the most dignified manner, "The meeting is called to order." Then each girl smoothed down her frock and sat up very straight waiting to hear what should come next. "The real object of our club," Agnes began, "is to find ways of being kind to our schoolmates, but we are going to do other things to entertain ourselves, things like bringing new games into the club and any new book we find particularly interesting. If anyone can write a story she is to do that, and if anyone hears anything particularly interesting to tell she is to save it up for the meeting. It has been proposed by Mrs. Conway that we call the club the Kindly Club or the Golden Rule. Celia, we'd better take a vote on the name. You might hand around some slips of paper and let the members write their choice. There is one thing about it; if we call it the Golden Rule Club, we can always refer to it as the G. R., and that will be rather nice, I think. However, you all must vote as you think."

There were not quite enough pencils, but by judicious borrowing they made out and the slips were handed in and gravely counted by Celia. "There are four votes for Golden Rule, and two for Kindly," she announced.

"Then it is a majority for Golden Rule, so the name of the club is the Golden Rule Club, or the G. R., whichever you choose to say when you are speaking of it. Now, let me see, oh, yes. We are the charter members. We haven't any charter but we can have one, I reckon. I'll get one ready for next time. Now, we must have rules. I haven't thought them all out, but I have two or three. We begin with the Golden Rule: 'Do unto others as ye would they should do unto you'; Mrs. Conway said we might head the list with that, for there was nothing better. Of course we all forget sometimes, but we mustn't any more than we can help. If we see a chance to do a kindness to any of our schoolmates we

19

must do it, no matter if we don't like her, and we must try not to get mad with any of the girls. We must be nice to the teachers, too. You see it is a school club and affects all in the school. We big girls mustn't be hateful to you younger ones and you mustn't be saucy to us."

"Oh, dear," sighed Edna, "it's going to be pretty hard, isn't it?"

"I don't believe it is going to be as much fun as the other girls' club," complained Dorothy.

"Oh, yes it is. You wait and see," said Agnes. "After a while everyone of them will be dying to come into ours."

"Oh, Agnes, I don't believe a bit of that," said Dorothy.

"Oh, but you see we are going to have very good times, you forget that part. The kind word part is only when we are having dealings with our schoolmates and all that. We don't have to do just that and nothing else. For example, I have the loveliest sort of story to read to you all just as soon as the business part of the meeting is over, and then we are to have refreshments."

"Oh, good!" there was emphatic endorsement of this.

"There ought to be fines, I suppose," Agnes went on. "Let me see, what shall we be fined for? I shall have to get some light upon that, too, but I think it would be a good plan that any girl who voluntarily stirs up a fuss with another at school must pay a fine of not less than one cent. What do you think of that, Celia?"

"I should think that might be a good plan though I expect we shall all turn Quakers if we continue the club."

Agnes laughed. "It does look that way. At all events we are to thank Clara Adams for it all. Her club is founded on unkindness and if we want to be a rival, Mrs. Conway says we must have ours founded on kindness."

"Do you know anything about her club?" asked Jennie.

"I know a little. I believe only girls who live in a certain neighborhood can belong to it. All others are to be turned down, and are to be left out of the plays at recess. It is something like that, I was told. However, we don't care anything about those poor little sillies. We shall enjoy ourselves much more. I think we'd better not attend to any business to-day or we shall not have time for anything else. Have you made the minutes, Celia?"

"Yes, I think I have, and if I haven't everything I can get you to tell me afterwards."

"I suppose we should vote for the officers," said Agnes, after a moment's thought.

"Oh, no, don't let's," said Edna, anxious for the story. "We all want you for president and Celia for secretary, don't we, girls?"

"All in favor of making Miss Agnes Evans president of the club will please rise," sang out Celia, and every girl arose to her feet. "That's unanimous enough," said Celia. "Now all in favor of my being secretary will please rise." Another unanimous vote followed this and so the matter was speedily settled.

Then Agnes produced a manuscript paper and read them the most delightful of stories which was received with great applause. Then she whispered something to Dorothy who nodded understandingly, retired to the back of the attic and returned with two plates, one of delicious little cakes and the other of caramels to which full justice was done.

"What about the places of meeting and the refreshments?" asked Celia. "It isn't fair for you always to furnish them and don't you think we should meet at different houses?"

"Perhaps so, only you see it would be hard for us to go into the city on Saturdays after coming out on Friday, and you see Jennie lives in town."

"Oh, but Mack can always bring me out in the motor car," said Jennie, "though of course I should love to have you all come in to my house and so would mamma like it."

"Well, we'll meet at your house, Celia, the next time," said Agnes, "and after that at Mrs. MacDonald's. We can, can't we, Margaret?"

"Oh, yes, I am sure she will be perfectly delighted. She is so pleased about the club, anyhow."

"Then in the meantime we can be making up our minds about your house, Jennie," said Agnes.

"I wish we had some little song or a sentence to close with," said Celia.

"We can have. We can do all those things later. I think we have done a great deal for one day, don't you all think so?"

"Oh, my, yes," was the hearty response. "It has been perfectly lovely."

"We might sing, 'Little Drops of Water,' for this time," proposed Edna, "as long as we haven't any special song yet."

"That will do nicely, especially that part about 'little deeds of kindness.' We're going to sing. All rise." And the meeting was closed, the members groping their way down the attic stairs which by now were quite dark. But the effect of the club was to be far-reaching as was afterward shown, though it was little suspected at the time of its formation.

CHAPTER IV

A THANKSGIVING DINNER

The first direct effect of the club was far from pleasant to Edna, for she forgot all about studying a certain lesson, and did not remember about it till she and Dorothy met at school on Monday morning, and then she was overcome with fear lest she should be called upon to recite something of which she knew scarcely anything. However, by dint of peeps at the book between whiles, after devoting to it all the time she had before school was called to order, she managed to get through the recitation, yet not without many misgivings and a rapid beating of the heart when Miss Ashurst called upon her. Edna was always such a conscientious child about her lessons that Miss Ashurst rather overlooked the fact that upon this occasion she was not quite as glib as usual, and she took her seat with a feeling of great relief, determining that she would not forget her lessons another Saturday.

There was more than one opportunity that day to exercise the rule of the G. R. Club, and the girls of the Neighborhood Club, as they called theirs, were a little surprised at the appearance of good-will shown by the others.

"Oh, I know just what they are up to," Clara Adams told her friends; "they want to get in with us and are being extra sweet. I know that is exactly their trick. Don't you girls pay any attention to them. Of course we could let Jennie Ramsey in, because she lives on our street, but the others, we couldn't any more than we could Betty Lowndes or Jessie Hill."

"Well, it seems to me if they are good enough for Jennie Ramsey to go with they are good enough for us," returned Nellie Haskell.

"No, I'm not going to have them," replied Clara, "and if you choose to go over to them, Nellie Haskell, you can just make up your mind that I'll have no more to do with you." So Nellie succumbed although she did smile upon Dorothy when the two met and was most pleasant when Edna offered to show her about one of the lessons.

Agnes advised that the girls make no secret of their club. "It is nothing to be ashamed of, I am sure," she said, "and if any of the girls want to join it I am sure they are quite welcome to." And indeed it did appeal so strongly to some of the older girls that before the week was out several new members were enrolled, and it was decided to change the time of meeting to Friday afternoon so that those in the city might have their convenience considered while the girls living in the country could easily stay in till a later hour.

The little girls felt themselves rather overpowered by the coming into their ranks of so many older members, but on the other hand they felt not a little flattered at being important enough to belong to the same club, so as the rule worked both ways it made it all right, especially as Betty Lowndes and others were admitted and were no older than themselves.

"They may have more in number," said Clara when she was told of how the club was increasing, "but we are more exclusive, my mother says."

This remark made its impression as Clara intended it should, though Nellie looked wistfully across at where half a dozen little girls were joyously eating their lunch and discussing the good times the elder girls were planning. "You know," Agnes had told them, "if you want to become a junior branch of the same club it will be perfectly easy for you to do it. At the end of a month you can decide, though Helen Darby and Florence Gittings agree with me that there is no reason why we shouldn't all hang together. It will be more convenient for one thing and we can take turns in arranging the entertainment part. I don't see why we all shouldn't enjoy some of the same kind of things."

"Oh, we'd much rather stay in," replied Edna. "At least I would."

"I would! I would!" came from all the others.

Although there is a high and marked difference between fifteen and eight or nine, in most matters, in this of the club there appeared to be a harmony which put them all on the same footing. The older sisters were more ready to help the younger ones with their lessons while the younger ones were more eager to run on errands or to wait on the older ones, in consequence there was a benefit all around.

Of course Miss Ashurst and Mr. Horner were by no means unaware of what was going on and they smiled to see how pleasant an atmosphere prevailed in the school all except in the unfortunate Neighborhood Club which they would have gladly disbanded. "It will probably die of its own discontent," said Miss Ashurst to the principal, "I give it just three months to exist for the girls are dropping out one by one."

Mr. Homer smiled and nodded his head. He was a man of few words yet very little escaped his keen eyes.

The next meeting of the G. R.'s was even more successful than the first. A number of things were discussed and the little girls learned many things that they had not known before.

"Suppose Clara Adams did want to come into the club or wanted to be friends I suppose we'd have to be kind to her," said Dorothy, a little regretfully.

"Of course you'd have to be kind to her," said Helen Darby, "but you wouldn't have to clasp her around the neck and hang on her words, nor even visit her. One can be kind without being intimate."

This was putting it in rather a new light and the little girls looked at one another. They had not easily distinguished the difference before this.

"The same way about Mr. Horner," Helen went on, "you don't have to get down and tie his shoes, but if you do have a chance to do something to make things pleasanter for him, why just trot along and do it." And Helen nodded her head emphatically.

"Dear oh, me," sighed Florence, "we are getting our standards way up. I should probably fall all over myself if I attempted to do anything for him. I am almost scared to death at the mere thought."

"He won't bite you," replied Helen, "and you don't have to get close enough to him to comb his eyebrows. What I mean is that we can 'be diligent and studious' as the old copy-books used to have it, speak well of his school, and not carry tales home that will make our families think we are martyrs and that he is an ogre, or someone to be feared constantly."

"Helen Darby! I'd like to know who has been giving you all these new ideas," said Florence.

"Why, I think Mrs. Conway started them by the way she talked to Agnes, and I have a modest claim to some brains of my own, so I thought out the rest and talked it over with father who put things very clearly before me, and showed me that school-girls are half the time silly geese who seem to think their teachers are created for the mere purpose of making their lives miserable. Father said that the shoe was usually on the other foot, and that the girls were much more liable to make the teachers' lives miserable. That set me a-thinking. Let me remark in passing that father says he thinks our club is great, and he wants to have a hand in furnishing the entertaining some time."

This announcement made quite a ripple of excitement, for Mr. Darby did nothing by halves and it was expected that there would be a good time for the G. R.'s when they met at Helen's house.

Edna kept in mind what had been said about Uncle Justus and before very long came an opportunity to prove her powers of doing him a kindness. It was just before Thanksgiving that Mrs. Conway came in one Thursday afternoon to see Aunt Elizabeth and of course her own two little daughters as well. Edna sat very close to her mother on the sofa, her hand stroking the smooth kid glove she wore.

It was a queer thing to have her mother for company, but it was very delightful, too.

"I hope you and Uncle Justus can come out to take Thanksgiving dinner with us," said Mrs. Conway to her aunt.

"Thank you, my dear, but I am afraid it is impossible," was the response. "I long ago promised to go to sister Julia's, and hoped Justus would go, too, but he insists that he cannot possibly take the time, for it is something of a trip. He says he has some school papers he must attend to, and moreover, has promised to address a meeting in the afternoon, so that it will be impossible."

"I am very sorry," returned Mrs. Conway, "for we had quite counted on you both. Perhaps Uncle Justus can take the time to come to us even if he cannot go so far as Aunt Julia's."

Mrs. Homer shook her head. "I am afraid not, but you can ask him. Julia will be greatly disappointed, but you know Justus is nothing if not conscientious and if he has made up his mind he ought not to go, nothing will alter his decision."

"What time is his meeting?" asked Mrs. Conway.

"At half past two, I believe."

"Oh, dear, then I am afraid it will be difficult for him to get to us, or rather to get away. We are to have dinner at two rather than in the evening, partly on account of the children and partly on account of the maids, to whom I have promised the time after they have finished the necessary work. There is a train at two-forty-five, but that would be too late, and it takes nearly an hour by the trolley cars."

"Then I am afraid he will have to dine alone," said Mrs. Horner, "I don't suppose he has ever done such a thing in his life as that, but it cannot be helped. Julia has few opportunities of seeing her family and he insists that I must not think of disappointing her on his account."

Edna listened very soberly to all this, and when it was learned later that nothing could alter Uncle Justus's decision, she felt very sorry for him. She took occasion to open up the subject herself that afternoon. "Uncle Justus," she asked, "did you ever eat Thanksgiving dinner alone?"

Uncle Justus looked at her over his spectacles. "Well, no, I cannot say that I ever did."

"Shall you like to do it?"

"No, I do not believe I shall particularly enjoy it, but duty must come before pleasure, you know."

"I wish you were going to have dinner with us."

"That would be very agreeable to me, but I fear I cannot think of it upon this occasion."

Edna sighed. She had hoped he might reconsider it. When he had left the room she went out into the kitchen to see Ellen of whom she was very fond. "Ellen," she said "are you going to stay in and cook Uncle Justus's Thanksgiving dinner for him?"

"I am thot. It'll not be much of a job I'll be havin' ayther."

"Why! Isn't he going to have a real Thanksgiving dinner?"

"She was tellin' me this mornin' thot it would be aisy, and I cud have me afthernoon the same as usual, for he'd not be in. Says she, 'a bit av a chicken will do and ye can make a pumpkin pie the day before, so what with a few pertaties and a taste of stewed tomats he'll do bravely."

"Oh dear!" Edna sighed again as she thought of all that would be served at her own home table. Her little face wore a very serious and troubled look every time she looked at Uncle Justus that evening and the next day at recess she unburdened her heart to Dorothy and Jennie. These three always ate their lunch together and they took this opportunity for many a confidence.

"Girls," Edna began smoothing down her frock and folding her hands. "I have a chance to do Uncle Justus a kindness and I can't make up my mind to do it. I'm afraid I'm awfully selfish."

Dorothy laughed. "I'd like to see anybody who's less so, wouldn't you, Jennie?"

"I certainly would. Edna, tell us about it."

"Well, you see Uncle Justus has things to do so he can't go with Aunt Elizabeth to her sister's and he hasn't even time to come to us for Thanksgiving, and he will have to eat his dinner all alone, unless—unless I stay and keep him company."

"Oh Edna, and you couldn't be with your family last year because you were here." Dorothy's tones were almost awe-stricken.

"I know, and of course I am dying to be at home, and that's where the being selfish comes in, I keep thinking how I should hate to eat my dinner alone and every time I look at Uncle Justus I feel so sorry for him I can hardly stand it, then when I think of not going home I feel so sorry for myself I can scarcely stand that."

Both girls were silent. They saw the opportunity for heroic sacrifice as well as Edna did, but they could not advise her either way; it was too weighty a question, though Jennie ventured, "If he is going to be busy all the time you would be all by yourself except at dinner."

"Yes," Edna nodded, "and Ellen is going out after she gets the dishes done, but I suppose I could go home after that. She could put me on the trolley and I'd get home in an hour. I thought about that."

"So, then it wouldn't be like staying all day, would it?" said Dorothy, brightening a little as she saw this much light upon the matter.

"Yes, of course that would make a great difference," returned Edna.

"Or," Jennie had a sudden brilliant thought. "Oh, Edna, I wonder if you couldn't come to my house and stay all night with me. I should be so delighted to have you and I know mother would, too. We aren't to have our Thanksgiving dinner till six, so you could have two."

Edna looked quite happy as this plan was suggested. What girl of nine does not delight in such an experience as spending the night with a friend? The thought of two Thanksgiving dinners, though one might be rather a frugal one, had its charm, too. "I think that would be perfectly lovely," she said, then after a moment's thought, "but you must ask your mother first and I'll ask mine."

"I'll ask her as soon as I go home and will tell you at the club meeting this afternoon, and then you can ask your mother when you get home and let me know on Monday. I just know what mother will say before I ask her."

Then the bell rang and recess was over, but Edna returned to her lessons very happy at this solution of what had been a matter of deep thought. It turned out just as Jennie had prophesied, for she brought a veritable invitation to Edna that afternoon in the shape of a little note, and she further said that Mrs. Ramsey meant to make sure by writing a formal request to Mrs. Conway, therefore Edna considered the matter as good as settled.

She was full of the subject that afternoon when she reached home. It was quite dark although she and the others had taken the train which brought them more quickly. The club meetings were so interesting that it was hard to get away in time, but Mrs. Conway was on the watch as the girls came in the gate. Of course Edna had told Celia about all this, and indeed it had been talked over at the club, all the girls agreeing that it was a perfectly lovely thing for Edna to do, so she came in quite exalted by all the approval.

However, when she told her tale and her mother saw that it was a case of genuine desire to do a good deed, and that in the beginning it had appeared in the light of a heavier sacrifice than could be made easily, she felt that she could allow the child to do as she wished, being sure that it was not in a spirit of self-righteousness. And so, on the evening before Thanksgiving after Uncle Justus had returned from seeing Mrs. Horner safely on her journey to her sister's, he saw a little figure watching for him at the window.

"Well, well, well, little girl," he said, "how is this? I thought you would have been at home before now."

"I'm not going till Friday," replied Edna smiling up at him. "I'm going to stay and have Thanksgiving dinner with you."

"What? What? What?" Uncle Justus frowned and shook his head, but he took off his spectacles and wiped them very vigorously.

"Yes, I am." Edna was very decided. "Mother said I might, and oh, Uncle Justus, she knew Aunt Elizabeth would be away and she thought maybe you and I would like some of our Thanksgiving, so she has sent some of her goodies, and we're going to have a lovely time. I am going to help Ellen set the table and wipe the dishes."

"But, my child, I cannot allow it. No, no, no."

"Oh, but, please." The more Uncle Justus denied, the more anxious was Edna.

"But, my child, it would be selfish and inconsiderate of me in the extreme to take you away from your family on a holiday. I know what it means to little people to have such treats, and to an old fellow like me it will not make such a difference."

"But you told me you had never had a Thanksgiving dinner alone."

"That is quite true, but it is no reason why I should call upon a little girl like you to give up the holiday to me."

"Don't you want me to stay?" asked Edna wistfully, and feeling a little hurt lest after all, her sacrifice was not really needed.

Then Uncle Justus did a rare thing. He sat down, put his arm around her and kissed her on the cheek. "My dear little girl," he replied, "if that is the way you feel, I can only say that I am delighted beyond measure that you want to stay, and you will give me a greater cause for thanksgiving than I have expected or deserved," and he drew her to his knee.

Edna smiled as she wondered what Florence Gittings, or any of the other girls, for that matter, would say if they could see her then so extremely near the fierce eyebrows.

"But what will you do in the afternoon?" asked Uncle Justus after a moment. "I must go out early, you see."

"I know that. At first I thought I would get Ellen to put me on the cars to go home. It would be quite safe, for I have gone so many times, but Jennie Ramsey and her mother have invited me to come there to stay all night. I'll come back here on Friday, if you would like me to, Uncle Justus. I could stay till Aunt Elizabeth comes home."

Uncle Justus was silent for a moment. He smoothed her hair thoughtfully and then he said gently. "Your mother very kindly has asked me to spend the week end with you all, so suppose we go out together on Friday afternoon. I can take my papers with me and do my necessary work on Saturday there as well as here. Your little club meets on Friday afternoon, doesn't it? I will meet you and Celia at the station in time for the four-thirty train, which is the one you usually take, isn't it?"

Edna was surprised that Uncle Justus should know all this about the club and the time of their going home, but she didn't say so. "I think that will be a very nice plan," she told him. "I'll come back here on Friday morning and have dinner with you, and then I can go to the club meeting. It is to be at Helen Darby's this time, and that is very near, you know." The twilight gathered about the two and in the dim light Uncle Justus did not appear in the least a person to stand in awe of, for when Ellen came to call them to supper she was surprised to see the little girl still sitting on the old man's knee, his arm around her and her head on his shoulder.

30

CHAPTER V

IN A BLIZZARD

The enjoyment of helping Ellen, of setting the table and of being consulted on such important subjects as whether the best china and the finest tablecloth should be used almost made up to Edna for being away from home on Thanksgiving day. The basket sent by Mrs. Conway contained several things which made the dinner much more of a feast than it would otherwise have been, for there was a jar of tomato soup, a small chicken pie with scalloped leaves and little balls of crust on top, some delicious pickles, a glass of currant jelly and another of cranberry sauce. Margaret had brought in a bunch of cut flowers from Mrs. MacDonald's greenhouse, the day before and these set in the middle of the table were a lovely ornament.

"It's the foinest lookin' table iver I saw in this house," said Ellen when Edna called her in to see. "What was it yez were sayin' about thim little toasty crusts for the soup. I'd be afther makin' thim if I cud know wanst."

"Oh, I can tell you just how," said Edna, "for I have watched our cook make them." She felt very important to be overseeing this piece of cookery and went in to call her uncle, feeling very much pleased at what had been accomplished.

"Well, well, well," exclaimed Uncle Justus, "this does look like holiday times. Who did all this?"

"Ellen and I," Edna told him, "and it was lots of fun."

Uncle Justus nodded. "I dare say," he said with a smile, as he sat down.

It was really a merrier repast than Edna had ever eaten under that roof, for instead of eating his dinner in silence as he generally did, Uncle Justus was quite talkative and actually attempted to joke once in a while. When Ellen was taking away the plates before she served the dessert, the old gentleman arose. "I think," he said, "that this is just the occasion to open that jar of ginger Captain Doane sent me awhile ago." So he went to his own special cupboard, unlocked the door and brought forth the wicker bound ginger jar which had been there several weeks, and it is safe to say Edna was given her share.

"A famous dinner," said Uncle Justus as he rose from the table. "I can't remember that I ever had a pleasanter one, and I have you to thank for it, my dear. Now, I am afraid I shall have to go to my meeting, but I know you have an agreeable plan for the evening, so I do not feel the reluctance in leaving that I should otherwise."

Edna helped him on with his overcoat, handed him his walking stick and saw him off, standing in the door, and hoping he would look back. He did this

31

giving her a smile and nod as she waved her hand. Then she went back to Ellen and together they did the dishes very carefully. After this both must get dressed, and an hour later they were about to start when the bell rang and Ellen opened the door to Jennie Ramsey.

"I thought I'd just come for you in the motor car," she said. "Mother said Mack could take us for a little ride in the fresh air so we would have a better appetite for dinner."

This was quite exciting, for Edna's opportunities for riding in an automobile were not many.

The magnificence of the Ramsey's dinner far outdid Aunt Elizabeth's, but Edna did not enjoy it one whit the more, although it was very delightful to be served by a man in livery, and to have such exquisite china and glass to look at during the meal. The child felt a little shy in the presence of so many strangers, and had little to say. Moreover, she had too often been told by Aunt Elizabeth that "little children should be seen and not heard" for her not to remember she must not chatter. Really the best time came when she and Jennie went up to bed when Jennie showed her all her treasures, her pretty room and her rows of books. They became very confidential as they snuggled down under the covers, and when Mrs. Ramsey came in to kiss them both good-night, Edna felt much happier than had seemed possible she could be when she first considered that she must spend the day and night away from her mother.

The club meeting at Helen Darby's the next day was a fine affair, too, for Mr. Darby had provided an entertainment which pleased them all. A wonderful juggler did all sorts of curious tricks and a young man sang the drollest of songs. Then, too, the refreshments were unusually good. It had been made an inviolable rule that not more than three articles were to be served, but when there were ice cream, delicious cakes and bon-bons, surely these were quite enough.

"You see," said Helen in explanation, after some of the girls had protested, "father said this was a holiday meeting and it might be a little more elaborate, he thought."

Uncle Justus took Edna and Celia home that evening, and if he did not enjoy his visit it was not the fault of the girls. It is probable the old gentleman had rarely had such attentions and such a fuss made over him. He was invited to the Evans's to supper on Saturday and to Mrs. MacDonald's to dinner on Sunday. He was taken to drive; he was invited to walk, and really was quite overcome by all this thought of him from the members of the G. R. Club.

Monday morning saw everyone but Celia back at school. Celia having had too much Thanksgiving, or too much something was not able to go, and indeed, had to remain at home for the entire week, and it seemed very much like the old days to Edna when she had to stay at Uncle Justus's without her sister. Aunt Elizabeth returned home on Monday afternoon, quite "smoothed out" Edna told her mother afterward. So the week sped along in the old way till Friday afternoon.

It had begun to snow a little when Edna started out to the club meeting which was held at Florence Gittings's. The little girl had no fear, however, for she expected to meet Dorothy and Agnes and go home with them, but for some reason neither was present. Later on it was learned that Mr. Evans had called for them at their aunt's and had taken them home fearing a heavy storm would prevent their going later. A telegram which they sent to Edna at Florence Gittings's was not delivered till after the child had left the house.

"You aren't going off by yourself," said Florence when the club meeting was over. It had seemed rather a poor little affair after the brilliancy of Helen's entertainment, and with both Agnes and Celia missing. However they had all done their best, but it broke up rather earlier than usual.

"Oh, I must go," said Edna. "I am sure Agnes and Dorothy will be at the railway station, and we can all go out together."

"But it is snowing so hard and the wind is making the snow drift," continued Florence.

"Oh, but the cars go all the way to the station. I won't have to walk, and very likely mother will send one of the boys, Cousin Ben, perhaps, to meet me."

"I wish we had a telephone," said Florence, "but we haven't, and I suppose you can telephone from the station if you want to."

"I might do that," said Edna.

"I think you'd better go back to your Uncle Horner's," suggested Helen.

"Oh, but—" Edna did not want to do this. A whole week at the school without Celia was about all she thought she could stand. "I shall do all right," she insisted. "I'm sure the girls will be at the station." So the others saw her depart without urging her further.

Owing to the snow which was drifting heavily, the cars were running much more slowly than usual, and when Edna reached the station her train had just gone. It was the train her father always took and she had hoped to see him. She decided to telephone and took out her purse to see what money she had. Alas! she had but ten cents, not enough for an out-of-town toll. She had her school ticket fortunately. Celia was the one who always carried the money for the expenses, and Edna remembered that her mother had told her to be sure to provide herself with enough. "If you find you run short," she told the child,

33

"either send down to your father for some change or borrow it from Aunt Elizabeth."

Edna would rather have done almost anything than borrow from Aunt Elizabeth and she had forgotten to look in her purse anyhow, before starting. "Even if I had," she told herself, "I would have thought I had enough for I didn't expect to need anything but car fare." The next train would leave at five, but as it was a short run Edna thought she might venture to take it, even though it might be dark when she reached the station. She could telephone to the house from there, if necessary. So she waited patiently till it should be time for her train to be ready and then she went out and took her seat. It was snowing desperately hard she noticed as they moved along, and the train stopped frequently, but at last she reached her own station and got off feeling very thankful to be this near home. She looked around; not a soul was there to meet her. She would have to telephone. She turned toward the waiting-room, but to her consternation found the door locked.

There was not a soul in sight. She stood still for a while. It was getting colder, and the snow was drifting and swirling around at a great rate. What should she do? The station master had probably gone home to his supper, for there were no more trains till nearly six o'clock from either direction. He had not counted on his presence being needed between whiles once he had seen to his freight and baggage, and he had gone to the back of the building where he lived.

It was not more than a ten minutes' walk to her home in good weather, and Edna at last thought she would venture. She pulled her hat down over her ears and her coat collar up around her neck and started. It was desperate walking here in the country where the sharp wind seemed to search out every unprotected part of the body. The snow nearly blinded her, and cut her face like a knife. Every little while she had to stop to get breath, and as she found the difficulties increasing she thought of all the stories she had heard of persons perishing in the snow a few yards from their own door-ways. "I wish I had gone back to Uncle Justus," she murmured. "Oh, dear, I don't believe I will ever get there."

The whiteness of the snow made it possible for her to see a little of the way when she first started, but as she went on and it grew darker she began to wonder if she were in the road. She brushed away the stinging flakes and looked around, peering into the darkness gathering around her. Through the blinding, hurrying flakes she could see twinkling lights here and there, and presently she located the piece of woods just beyond her own home, but it was far to the left, and she realized that she had turned into a by-road instead of keeping to the main one. The tears began to course down her cheeks when she appreciated how far she was from her own house. "I can never go back," she sobbed. "I can't. I am so cold and so tired, I'm afraid I can't get there. It would never do to stand still," she realized and presently she made up her mind to struggle on toward the nearest light a little ahead.

She bowed her head again and pressed on through the drifts, feeling her strength would do no more than get her to this refuge. At last it was reached, a little house, by the wayside, a tiny garden in front and a small cow-shed behind. Managing to get the gate open, Edna went upon the porch and knocked at the door.

It was opened by a little girl about her own age. "Why," she exclaimed, "who is it? I thought you were mother. Come right in out of the storm. Isn't it a dreadful one?"

Edna, scarce able to speak, tottered into the room, warm from a bright fire in a base-burner stove and cheerful by reason of a lighted lamp.

"You are all covered with snow," the little girl went on. "Do come to the fire and take off your hat and coat. You must be nearly frozen and I expect your feet are wet and cold. I'll take off your shoes."

She stooped down and began to unfasten the snowy shoes after removing the rubbers Edna had been fortunate enough to have put on.

In a moment the wanderer was able to tell her story, and to thank her little hostess for her attentions. "I don't know what I am going to do," she said. "I'm afraid I can't get home, and there isn't any way to send them word to come for me. Of course they will think I have stayed in the city. If I had known how bad the storm was going to be I would never have started, but I did want to see my mother."

"And I want to see my mother," replied her hostess. "She went down the road this morning to see my aunt who is ill, and she was coming back on this train that got in a little while ago, the train you must have come on."

"I didn't see anyone get off," Edna told her, "only two or three men who got into a wagon and drove off before I left the station. Most everyone I know comes out on the train before that, but I missed it, you see."

"Well, I am very glad to have you here," said the other. "If mother did not come on that train she won't come at all, I am sure, for the next ones don't stop at my aunt's station, and I should have been here all alone. What is your name?"

"My name is Edna Conway, and I live on the main road just this side of that piece of woods you see after you pass Mrs. MacDonald's. Hers is the big gray house with the greenhouses, you know."

35

"Oh, yes I know it very well. My name is Nettie Black. My mother and I live here just by ourselves since my father died."

"Oh," Edna felt very sorry that Nettie was fatherless, but she did not know exactly what to say about it. "Will your mother be worried about your being here alone?" she asked after a moment.

"I s'pose she will, but it can't be helped. I know she would have come if she could. I only hope my aunt isn't worse. I wish she could know I am not to be alone."

"And I wish, my mother knew I was safe," returned Edna. "I am sure, though, that she thinks I am at my uncle's in the city, and I hope she does think so."

"Are you quite warm, now?" asked Nettie. "If you are we will have some supper."

"Oh, you are very kind," returned Edna a little embarrassed. "I think it is very hard on you to have me come in this way like a stray cat."

Nettie laughed. "I like stray cats, and we always take them in. There is a lovely one in the kitchen, now, that we make a great pet of. He came to us so thin and miserable, but now he is as fat as butter."

"I'd love to see him," returned Edna, "and won't you let me help you get supper?"

"There isn't so very much to get," returned Nettie a little shamefacedly. "There is only bread and butter and what is left of the rice-pudding I had for dinner. We could toast the bread, and there's milk. If you don't mind my taking part of the milk for it, I could have milk-toast and we could drink cambric tea."

"I like cambric tea," replied Edna, "and I am very fond of milk-toast. Oh, dear, I am so thankful to be here instead of out in the cold."

"I am thankful, too. I'll go out and make the toast. Will you come?"

Edna was pleased enough to do this, to make the acquaintance of the big black cat, and to help make the toast. "I don't see how you will ever know how to make the dip part," she said to Nettie.

"Oh, but I do know. Mother taught me, and I can do it very well. The great thing is not to let the milk burn and to put in only the least little bit of thickening."

Edna watched the process admiringly. Nettie was so very expert and bustled around like an experienced housekeeper. The house was very small, only two rooms downstairs and two up, with an attic over all, but everything was neat and clean, and the dishes, of course, were set out in an orderly manner upon a white tablecloth. The dish of smoking toast flanked by the rice pudding made an excellent meal. Nettie poured the tea and served her guest in the most hospitable way. They ate their meal in the front room before the fire, and now that she was warmed and was no longer hungry, Edna began to be interested in her surroundings. It was a plainly furnished room, a faded carpet on the floor, an old-fashioned sofa against one wall, a claw-footed mahogany table against the other, a bookcase between the windows. One or two engravings hung on the wall and a dingy portrait in an old frame. The chairs matched the sofa, one being a comfortable rocker with cover of haircloth.

After they had washed the supper dishes, Nettie made ready for the night by putting more coal on the fires and carefully barring the shutters and doors below. Then with a small lamp in her hand she escorted her guest to the upstairs room. It was rather chilly and was also plainly furnished, though the old-fashioned four-poster bed was made up neatly, and the high bureau showed a clean cover. The wind howled and whistled around the house, the sharp snow crystals clicked against the panes, but as Edna crept under the covers she could feel only thankful that she had this shelter and was soon asleep with Nettie beside her already in the land of Dreams.

CHAPTER VI

COUSIN BEN TO THE RESCUE

The next morning when Edna opened her eyes she saw a white world. Trees, fences, roofs, were covered with snow. It was banked up in great drifts along the road. The path to the gate was so deeply snowed under that it was an impossibility to think of getting from the house. At the back it was no better. The two little girls looked rather sober.

"I wonder if mother can get home to-day," was the first thought in Nettie's mind, and, "I wonder if I can get home to my mother," was that in Edna's.

It seemed rather forlorn to think of facing the day without some older person, but Nettie bravely went to work to do her best. First she went down into the cellar for coal which she lugged up to put on the two fires. Edna came down to find her busily taking up the ashes.

"Oh, how do you know what to do to make the fires burn?" she asked.

"Oh, I know, for mother has told me, and I often do this for her. The kitchen fire is easy enough but it is hard to lift the coal bucket up high enough to get the coal into the other stove."

"I can help," said Edna. So together they managed.

"Now, I must see what there is for breakfast," said Nettie. "I think there are two eggs, and the hens must have laid more, but I can't get out to hunt them till a path is made. I think there is still a little milk, for it didn't take much for the cambric tea, and we can have more of that. Then there is bread enough and butter. We can boil the eggs."

This they did, Edna watching the clock very carefully to see that they were not over done. They concluded to toast the bread, and made a pretty fair breakfast, though it was not a very hearty one, Edna thought. There was a little of the milk toast left which they warmed up to give to the cat who must miss his morning's milk, as the milkman had not appeared.

"I don't suppose he will get here at all," said Nettie a little anxiously. She was wondering what she could give her guest for dinner if it should be so that her mother did not return. She set to work in a very housewifely way to tidy up the house, Edna helping all she could. Then they stationed themselves by the window to see if by any chance there might be someone coming along whom they could hail. But the road was not much frequented and there was not a footstep nor a track in the deep snow. Only the smoke from neighboring chimneys gave any evidence of life. Once they heard sleigh-bells in the distance and concluded that the main road was being used.

"I wish I could get out to feed the chickens," said Nettie after a while. "I am afraid they will be hungry." She went to the back door to view the prospect, and tried to shovel away some of the snow, but it was slow work. Edna brought another shovel and together they managed to clear a few feet of the path, but it was very wearying and they soon had to give it up.

Then they went back to the window, but the monotony was not relieved by any change in the face of things and so they determined that it was rather stupid to stand there. Nettie brought down her two dolls and they played with these for a while, but keeping house in a make believe way was not so exciting when there was the reality close at hand, and they decided that paper dolls would be more entertaining.

"I think there is a fashion book upstairs in the garret," said Nettie, "and we can take that. Mother said I might have it."

Edna followed her up into the attic and they found the book, took it down into the front room and began to make their selections and cut out paper dolls till it suddenly dawned upon Nettie that it was time for another meal. She laid down her scissors with a sigh. "I really don't know what we shall have for dinner," she said. "Mother was going to bring something back with her. I shall have to rummage."

She went into the little pantry, Edna following. "There are two potatoes, but they aren't very big," she said, "and there is some codfish. I might make some codfish balls if I knew how. Do you know, Edna?"

"I think they are made of fish and potatoes, aren't they?"

"Yes, but I don't know how much fish and how much potato, besides I am afraid there aren't potatoes enough. I suppose we shall have to give that up. Oh, here are some more eggs; that is fine. If I could find some ham or some bacon we could have ham and eggs, and that would be very good." But nothing of this kind could be discovered and Nettie brought out the potatoes, laid them on the table and said rather ruefully, "It seems to me that we aren't going to have much dinner. There isn't another thing except sugar and tea and such things."

"There might be rice," said Edna with a sudden thought of Aunt Elizabeth's desserts.

"Why, of course, and rice and brown sugar are very good indeed. I am so glad you thought of it. I know there must be rice." She went back to the pantry and presently came out with a box in which she had discovered the rice. "I'll get the eggs and we can have them fried," she remarked, "they will seem more like meat that way."

"And we can have the potatoes baked because they will be easier to do," said Edna.

Nettie made another visit to the pantry. "I've found something else," she called.

"What?" asked Edna going to the door.

"Two apples. Now, I am sure that is every blessed thing."

"Well," said Edna cheerfully, "I think we are very lucky to find so much."

"I must put the potatoes in the oven right away," declared Nettie, "for it takes them a good while to bake. I will put on some water for the rice, too. I wonder how much rice I should take. Have you any idea?"

"No, I haven't, but I should think we will want quite a good deal, we haven't very much else, have we?"

"No, we have not. I will take a large cupful. It swells up so, I should think that might do. You soak it first, I think." She measured out a full cup of the rice, poured some water over it, washed it and then set it to soak till the water should boil. The potatoes were put in the oven and then the two went back to the next room. "It won't take the rice as long as it does the potatoes, I am sure," said Nettie, "and the water will have to boil first."

They returned to the paper-dolls, becoming quite interested in them till presently they heard a great sputtering, and running out found the water was boiling over. "I'll put on the rice now," said Nettie, "for I am getting hungry, aren't you?"

"Well, yes, a little," acknowledged Edna.

Nettie was rather uncertain as to what she should cook the rice in, and next, how much water she should pour over it, but after some discussion it was decided, and they went back to set the table. "Doesn't it seem funny to be keeping house just like grown-ups?" said Edna. "I never knew how much trouble it was before, did you, Nettie?"

"I knew, but I didn't think about it, I suppose," returned Nettie. "We will pile up our dolls and papers over here on this other table and then they will be easy to get at when we want them. I wish the milkman had come, for I really don't know what to give to Tippy. We haven't any meat. To be sure he will eat most anything, but I am afraid he will go hungry to-day."

"Couldn't you give him an egg and some bread or some rice, if we have enough."

"I could do that, I suppose. I hope there will be rice enough, but it is very hard to tell when you aren't acquainted with such a thing as the boiling and swelling of it."

"Oh, I smell something burning," cried Edna, "and something is making a funny popping noise." They flew to the kitchen to see that the rice had burst all bounds and was dancing out of the saucepan all over the hot stove, puffing and popping at a great rate.

"Oh, dear," exclaimed Nettie. "I never saw so much rice come from one cupful. Could you believe it? Why, it has taken up all the water and the saucepan is full up to the top besides all that is on the stove. Oh, dear, I wish I knew just how to cook it."

"Haven't you a cook book?" asked Edna with a quick suggestion of what might help out the question.

"Why, of course mother has one. I will set this off and go hunt it up."

The book was found on the shelves and the two put their heads together to discover the best way to boil rice. "I think this seems the easiest way," said Nettie, pointing to one of the pages of the book, "but I hope it won't hurt it to wait, for I'll have to put on more water to boil. It says to have a great deal of water and keep it boiling like mad."

After some time the rice was transferred to another and larger saucepan and was soon boiling "like mad," then the eggs were fried and after a somewhat anxious and laborious period of time the dinner was pronounced ready.

"Oh, dear me, but it is hard work," said Edna sighing as the two sat down to partake of the meal which they had prepared after so much difficulty.

"Yes, it is hard work," agreed Nettie, "but we did it all ourselves, and the potatoes are really done and the rice looks all right."

"It looks fine," said Edna, "and so do the eggs. I don't mind their being broken a little; I don't see how you could dish them up without."

They had been so long in preparing the meal that they were quite starved and ate with a relish. "I'm glad there is more rice," said Nettie, "for now that I know what a little it takes to make a big dish I shan't be afraid of our starving while it lasts."

"Oh, dear," Edna put down her spoon, "you don't think we shall have to stay here alone for days, do you? The snow will have to melt after a while and the roads be cleared."

"It doesn't look much like it yet," returned Nettie.

"Oh, but it never, never, never could keep on like this." Edna was determined to be hopeful. "I'm going to believe someone will come this very afternoon, either your mother or somebody."

Her faith was not without foundation for along in the middle of the afternoon they heard jangling bells, and ran to the front window to see the milkman in a huge sleigh, his milk cans in the body of it. He plowed his way to the front door which was opened to him before he could knock.

"Oh, Mr. Snyder," said Nettie, "I am so glad you have come. We are all alone and we haven't a drop of milk."

"That so?" said Mr. Snyder. "I thought as much. It's pretty hard travelling and I've been hours getting around to my customers, but now the road is broken it won't be quite so hard getting back. I'd better leave you double quantity in case I'm late to-morrow."

"Oh, you are our milkman, too, aren't you?" said Edna. "You leave milk at Mrs. Conway's, don't you?"

"To be sure I do."

"And have you been there yet?"

"No, I'm on my way now. You're out a bit, you know, but what are you doing down here?"

Edna told him her tale in which he was much interested. "Well, I declare," he said. "Want me to take you home with me? I can bundle you in there with the milk cans, and I reckon you wouldn't freeze."

For a moment Edna thought she must accept this invitation, then she looked at Nettie. Suppose her mother should not come that evening, and she should be there at night all alone. "Couldn't you take Nettie, too?" she said.

"Why, certainly. The two of you aren't much more than two milk cans, and I'm sure you're not so big round."

"Oh, but suppose mother should come," said Nettie. "She would be so worried, and I must be here to keep up the fires."

"Then," said Edna firmly, setting her face against the temptation of the cheerful supper table at home, the dear mother arms, the greetings of the boys and all the rest of it. "I will tell you what I can do. I will write mother a little note and ask her if she can send somebody or find some way to get us something to eat, and I'll stay till your mother comes, Nettie."

"Oh, I think you are lovely to do that," answered Nettie.

"Could you wait a minute, Mr. Snyder?" asked Edna. "I won't write much."

"I'll wait," he said, "and if you will give me a shovel I'll make a path to your gate. I reckon you're right about staying, sissy. I've got two little girls of my own and I know I shouldn't like them to be left alone either one of them."

Edna hurried through her note which said: "Dear mother, I am with Nettie Black. She lives in the first little house on the side road on the way to the old mill. We are all alone for her mother hasn't come back. Please send us something to eat if you can, for we have nothing left but rice and milk. There may be eggs in the hen-house, but we can't get at them. I want to come but I'd better not. Your loving Edna."

The little note was safely stowed away in Mr. Snyder's pocket with a promise of sure delivery, and he went off, his horses plunging through the deep drifts up to their middles.

"I think you are just as good as you can be," said Nettie. "I don't feel as if I ought to let you stay, but I do hate the idea of being left all alone."

"I'd want you to stay with me if I were in your place," returned Edna remembering the G. R. Club. To be sure Nettie did not belong to her school, but she was quite as much one of those "others" to whom one should do as he would be done by.

"It really looks as if something had happened," remarked Edna. "When we see the path to the gate. I wish he had had time to make one at the back, too."

It was almost dark and they were about to turn from the window to light the lamp, when ploughing through the deep snow they saw someone coming down the road. They watched him eagerly. Except the milkman he was the first person they had seen that day. "He is coming this way," said Edna hopefully. "Oh, Nettie, I believe it is Cousin Ben. He has a basket and see how he has taken to the road where Mr. Snyder's sleigh went along." She watched for a few minutes longer. "It is Cousin Ben," she cried joyfully. "He is coming here. Light the lamp, Nettie, while I go let him in."

She hurried to the door to see Ben stamping off the snow from his feet. "Whewee!" he exclaimed, "but isn't this a sockdolager? I never saw such a storm? How are you Ande, my honey. Of all things to think of your being this near home and none of us knowing it."

"Then mother did think I was still at Uncle Justus's," said Edna.

"Just what she did. You rung a surprise on the whole of us, I can tell you."

He came in and set down the basket, took off his cap and overcoat and looked down at the two little girls with a smile.

"This is Nettie Black," Edna told him. "She has been so nice to me, and I don't know what would have happened if I had not been able to get to her house."

"Don't speak of it," returned Ben with a little frown and a shake of his head. "I'll sit down and warm myself and then you can tell me how this all happened."

He drew up to the fire, took Edna on his knee and she poured forth her tale. "Pretty tough," he said when she had completed her story. "I'm glad your mother didn't know you had started. Now, Miss Nettie if you will let me sleep on that big sofa I am going to stay right here till we can dig you out and your mother comes. There's a lot of provender in that basket and we'll be as jolly as they make 'em."

"Oh, but you can sleep upstairs," returned Nettie. "There is plenty of room."

"Good! Then upstairs be it. What was that about hens and eggs and things, Ande?"

"Oh, we can't get out to the hen-house, you know. We tried to make a path but it was too hard work for us so we gave it up."

"I should remark. Well, that will be done first thing in the morning, and I'll go see what I can find. Eggsactly, as it were. What about the fires? Any coal up here?"

"A little," Nettie told him. "We have carried up all we could at a time, but we couldn't bring enough for the fires to-night. We are going down to get more."

"You are going to do no such thing. Got a candle? Where are the coal scuttles? One of you hold the light and show me your coal bin and up comes your coal." Cousin Ben was already making for the cellar door.

Of course no one was going to be left out of this expedition and all three descended to the cellar, from which they presently came forth all laughing. It was certainly a cheering thing to have someone so willing to come to their aid. Next the basket was unpacked and it goes without saying that there were neither eggs nor rice for supper that night. Moreover, Tippy had such a feast of milk as well as other things as he had not seen for several days. Ben kept the little girls in such a state of giggle that they could scarcely do the dishes, but what with the labors of the day and the later excitement they were ready for bed early, and went up leaving Cousin Ben with a book before him. Later his light half wakened Edna, but as he closed the door between the rooms and she realized that he was there, she turned over with a sigh of content, feeling very safe and sleepy.

CHAPTER VII

DISTURBANCES

Sunday morning was bright and clear. It was so dazzlingly bright when the little girls arose that they thought it must be much later than it was. Cousin Ben, however, was already up and dressed and had been down some time when the two finally descended to the lower floor. This was made known by reason of the fires burning brightly and of there being a path cleared to the hen-house, while as many as a dozen eggs were in a bowl on the kitchen table.

"Oh, Cousin Ben," cried Edna, "what a lot you have done. It is so cosey and warm down here, and we won't have to wait at all for breakfast."

"I hope not," he returned, "for I'm hungry, for one. What are you going to have?"

Edna turned to Nettie who considered the question. It was a great occasion when there were two guests to be provided for. "As long as there are so many eggs," she said, "we can have muffins or something and some eggs. I could have some kind of breakfast food, too, I believe there's some oat-meal."

"Never mind the oat-meal," said Ben. "You get me out the flour and stuff and I'll make the muffins. There is a royal fire and I'll get them ready in three shakes of a sheep's tail."

"You?" Nettie looked amazed.

"Of course. Did you never hear of a man cook? I've served my apprenticeship, I can assure you. I'll make the coffee, too, if you have any."

"Oh, there is some already ground, in the basket mother sent," Edna assured him. "We don't drink it, but we can have cambric tea."

"All right, you go along and set the table, and I'll do the rest."

Nettie was rather glad to have the responsibility taken off her hands in this summary manner, though she said to Edna, "Do you think it is polite to let him do it all?"

"Why, certainly," replied Edna. "He does those things at home for his mother sometimes, for he has no sisters, and the boys have to pitch in and help when the servant goes out. He has told me all about it. And as for its being polite, I remember mother said it was always more polite to let your company do the thing which made them comfortable than to insist upon doing something for them that would make them uncomfortable."

46

Nettie considered this for some time before she quite took in the sense of it. She was a thin, demure little girl, not at all pretty, but with a kind face, big blue eyes and sandy hair. She was dressed very plainly, but her clothes were neat and simply made. She was not the kind of child Edna might have expected to find in such a little house.

The muffins turned out a great success, and Ben said his coffee just suited him. "I never saw fresher eggs than your hens lay," he said, looking at Nettie with a serious face.

"Of course, they are fresh," she returned, "when they were only laid yesterday."

"That's what I said," returned Ben, with gravity.

Edna laughed. She was used to Cousin Ben's ways, but Nettie was a little puzzled.

The breakfast was as merry an affair as the supper had been, and after it was cleared away there was a consultation upon what should be done next. "There's no use in thinking of church," said Ben. "We couldn't get there if we tried."

"And there are so few trains I don't suppose I can expect mother this morning," said Nettie.

"Better not expect her at all," replied Ben, "that is, not while the roads are so snowy. There is scarcely any use in even a sleigh while these drifts are so high. Ande, what is the use of a sleigh, anyhow?" he asked, turning to his cousin who saw a joke.

"You tell," she answered.

"Snow use" he replied. "Now, I'll go out and feed the hens, and then I'll put on my boots and start on the road again. I'll see what's going on at the house, and then I'll come back again." They watched him ploughing through the snow, but because he had been there and was coming back it seemed not lonely at all, though Nettie said, wistfully, she did hope her mother could come that day, and Edna hoped she could find a way of getting home.

Toward noon they saw a queer box-sleigh coming from the main road. They watched it interestedly from the window as it approached nearer and nearer. "I do believe it is mother," exclaimed Nettie, joyfully. And sure enough the sleigh did stop before the door, a man got out, and then helped a slight woman in black to alight. "It is mother," cried Nettie, running to the door, and presently she was in her mother's arms.

47

Then there were great explanations. Like the little girls, Mrs. Black had been snowed in, for her sister lived quite a distance from the station, but she had at last been able to get some one of the neighbors to bring her across, as he had to go to the doctor's, and was willing to take her the short distance further.

"If I had known how well cared for you would be," she told her daughter, "and that you were not alone at all, I should have been much less anxious. Certainly, we have a great deal to be thankful for."

Edna felt that she certainly had a great deal to be thankful for when a little later she saw a big black sleigh stop before the door. She recognized it as Mrs. MacDonald's, for it was driven by her coach-man, though in it sat Cousin Ben. He had come back as he promised, but in great state. And because Nettie's mother had returned he bore Edna off alone, after many good-bys and promises to see her new friend as often as she could.

"How did you happen to come in Mrs. MacDonald's sleigh?" she asked her cousin.

"Well, I will tell you. When I reached the house I found that Mrs. MacDonald had telephoned over to ask about all of you, and to see how Celia was. When she heard where you were and all about it, she said she would send over her sleigh and I could go for you and Nettie in it, and so as that seemed a good arrangement I was going to put it into execution. We had decided to leave a note for Mrs. Black in case she should get back to-day, so she wouldn't be worried."

"It's really much better this way," returned Edna, "for now she has her mother, and I will have mine."

It seemed a delightful home coming, and because the snow was still so deep there was the extra holiday on Monday, but by Tuesday all started off to school again. Mrs. MacDonald knew all about Mrs. Black, and said she was a very good woman, who had taken this little house in the country because she could live there more cheaply, and because in such a place as she could afford in the city her little daughter would not be surrounded by pleasant influences. Nettie went to the district school, and was such a little girl as Edna's parents would select as a companion for their daughter. So, Edna felt she had made quite a discovery, and planned all sorts of times with Nettie when the winter was over.

Matters went on at school uninterruptedly, until just before Christmas, when it was suddenly made known that Miss Ashurst was to be married, and that another teacher would take her place after the holidays. The G. R.'s got up a linen shower for the departing teacher, but the Neighborhood Club did nothing. Its numbers were dwindling, for when it was learned what good times the rivals had at their meetings, there was more than one deserter. For some reason, Clara Adams had picked out Edna as the prime cause of all this. She had never forgiven her for winning the doll at the fair the year before, and was likewise furiously jealous of her friendship for Jennie Ramsey. If Edna had been a less generous and sweet-tempered child, matters might have been much worse, but even as it was they were made bad enough.

No sooner had the new teacher appeared than Clara set to work to do everything in her power to make Edna appear to disadvantage, by all sorts of mean innuendoes, by sly hints, by even open charges, till the child was almost in tears over the state of affairs.

"I would just tell Miss Newman, so I would," said Dorothy indignantly, when a specially mean speech of Clara's came to her ears.

"Oh, but I couldn't be a tattle-tale," declared Edna.

"She'd better not say anything about you to me," returned Dorothy. "She knows better than that. I'd tell her a thing or two."

"If Uncle Justus knew, he would believe me and not Clara," said Edna. "I don't cheat in my lessons, and he knows I don't, whatever Clara may say, and I'm not the one who sets the girls up to mischief, you know I'm not."

"I know mighty well who it is," declared Dorothy, "and if this keeps up I shall tell, so I shall."

It did keep up till one morning the climax was reached when Miss Newman came into her school-room to find on the board a very good caricature of herself, with under it written: "Ugly, old Miss New," in scrawling letters. Clara came into the school-room late, and slipped into her seat after the exercises had begun. Miss Newman left the drawing on the board and made no reference to it, using a smaller board for what was necessary. She was far less attractive than Miss Ashurst, and had a dry little way with her, which many of the girls thought oldmaidish, but she was a good teacher, if not a very beautiful one. When the girls returned from recess, in place of Miss Newman at the desk stood Mr. Horner, his eyes fairly snapping with indignation, and his eyebrows looking fiercer than ever.

"Oh," whispered Dorothy, as she sank down into her seat by Edna's side. The rest of the girls looked pale and awe-stricken. Never before had they any recollection of Mr. Horner's coming into the room. Offenders were sometimes sent to him in the larger room, but this was a new experience.

There was complete silence, while Mr. Horner looked from one to the other as if he would search their very hearts. Some of the girls returned his gaze pleadingly, some dropped their heads, Clara Adams, with a little smile of indifference, began to play with her pencil. Mr. Horner glared at her. "Put that down!" he said, and she dropped it, though still wearing her impertinent little smile. "I wish to know," said Mr. Horner, "who was the first to arrive in this room this morning?"

"I was the last," spoke up Clara.

"You were not asked that," said Mr. Horner, turning upon her.

After quite a silence, Margaret arose. "I think I was the first, Mr. Horner," she said, and then sat down again.

"There was no one in the room when you came?"

"No, Mr. Horner."

"And was this on the board?" He pointed to the drawing.

"Yes, Mr. Horner."

"You did not do it?"

"No, Mr. Horner," then with a little catch of her breath, "I wouldn't do such a mean thing, not for nothing."

"Not for anything, I think you mean, Margaret," said Mr. Horner in gentler tones.

"Not for anything," repeated Margaret, meekly.

"Then, I shall have to ask each separately, and I expect a truthful answer," said Mr. Horner. He began putting the question, going from one to the next till every girl in the room had been questioned.

"It might have been one of the older girls," said Miss Newman, in an undertone to him.

Clara caught the words, as she was nearest. "I should think it would be very easy to know who did it," she said, "when there is only one of us girls who stays in the house."

"What do you mean by that?" asked Mr. Horner severely.

Clara was not daunted. "I mean that there is only one girl who can come into the school-room before the others can get here."

"Do you mean my niece? I should as soon think of suspecting Miss Newman herself." He looked over at Edna with a little reassuring smile. "However, as we do not seem to be making much headway I shall take other means of finding out who did this very unladylike and unkind thing." Then he gave them such a

50

lecture as none of them forgot and if the G. R.'s did not have their motto brought home to them on that occasion they never did. Then Mr. Horner returned to his own school-room and Miss Newman called one of the girls to clean off the board.

Nothing further was said of the matter, and Miss Newman went on as if it had never happened; but one day the last of the week, the girls were asked to illustrate in pencil drawings a story from their history lesson.

"Oh, Miss Newman, I couldn't possibly do it," exclaimed Dorothy. "I don't expect finished drawings," she replied, "and you may even make them as humorous as you choose, but I want some little attempt, no matter how slight. Mr. Horner has asked that you do your best, and I shall expect you to hand in something beside blank paper."

Dorothy and Edna both sighed. Neither one had the slightest idea of drawing and knew that their results would be absurd, but they labored away and finally with half deprecating, half amused expressions showed their drawings to one another. It was as much as they could do to keep from laughing outright, they were so very funny, but they signed their names in the corner as Miss Newman directed them to do, and handed them in. Then, Miss Newman took them into the next room. At the close of school, she said, "Mr. Horner wishes Clara Adams to stay after school; he wishes to see her about her drawing."

Clara perked up and looked around with a little smirk. So she was the prize draughtsman, and she remained with a perfectly good grace. However, it was a very different looking Clara who was led into the room the next morning by Mr. Horner. Her eyes were swollen with crying and she wore a rebellious expression when Mr. Horner announced, "Clara Adams wishes to make a public acknowledgment of her part in the rudeness directed against Miss Newman by the drawing you all saw on the board, and she will also make a public apology both to her teacher and to my niece."

Clara murmured something unintelligible and burst into tears. The only words the girls could make out were "I did it." It was the most terrible thing that had ever happened to any of them and Edna felt so sorry for the culprit that all resentment vanished altogether. She forgot entirely that she was included in the apology, if apology there was, and all morning she cast the most sympathetic looks across the room at Clara.

It came out later that the drawings were the proof of the child's guilt, for they were done in the same style as the caricature and because they were so much better than the rest it was evident that only Clara could have made the figure on the board. She had come very early, had slipped upstairs before anyone else and had gone out again to return later and thus hoped to avoid any suspicion. It happened, too, that Ellen saw her come in and go out again and this of course clinched the matter when she was brought face to face with the Irish girl who did not know her name but recognized the hat and coat she wore.

The affair made a great impression but somehow did not increase Miss Newman's popularity, for the idea of the drawings was hers and Clara could not forgive her for the position into which she had forced her, therefore she lost no opportunity of making it as unpleasant for her teacher as she could in the thousand and one ways a sly and unprincipled girl can, and her little pin-pricks were so annoying, that finally Dorothy and Edna, who had not particularly cared for the new teacher, began to stand up for her and to do as many kind things as they could. Perhaps the G. R. Club was mainly responsible for this, but at all events it made matters a little happier for the teacher.

As for Clara, Dorothy set her face against any sort of friendship with her, but it was not within Edna's heart to be unkind to anyone, and she made up her mind that she would meet Clara half way if ever the chance came.

Uncle Justus never mentioned the affair of the caricature to her, but she knew he had never the slightest belief that she had done it and his open approval of her before the whole class was very much valued. She had won her way into the hearts of most of the girls, and there were only two or three of Clara's most adoring adherents who still called her "a pet" and said she was at the bottom of all Clara's trouble. This seemed a very strange way to look at it, but poor Clara was so blinded by jealousy and rage that she saw nothing in the right light. Edna wondered if she would ever cease to dislike her, and insisted to Dorothy that they ought to try to persuade her to come into the club. "You see," she said, "if she could once find out what doing to others really means she maybe would get over all her hatefulness. Mother thinks so, and I'm not going to give up being nice to her if I get a chance."

"Well, you don't catch me," returned Dorothy. "I don't want to go with such a horrid story-teller as she is. I shouldn't think you would, either."

Edna said not a word, but still hoped.

CHAPTER VIII

THE FRIENDLESS FRIENDS

Margaret came to school in great excitement one Monday morning. "I'm going to have a party," she said to Edna. "I'll tell you all about it at recess."

The idea of Margaret's really having a party was most interesting when Edna remembered that it had been just a year since she was adopted by Mrs. MacDonald. She had improved very much in this time, both in speech and manner, and no happier child could be found than she. To be sure she had everything to make her happy, as Dorothy often said, a beautiful home, a kind mother and friends who took pains to make her forget how forlorn she had once been. She was very grateful for all these things, and rarely asked for anything more than was offered to her, so that Mrs. MacDonald was all the more ready to give her pleasures which she did not ask for.

Jennie and Dorothy were admitted into the little group which gathered to hear about the party. "Tell us all about it, Margaret," said Edna. "Just begin at the beginning."

"Well," said Margaret, "mother was saying to me on Saturday evening, 'Margaret, do you know it is almost a year since you became my own little daughter? Now I think we ought to celebrate the day of your coming to your home. What would you like to do?' So I thought and thought, and then I said, 'I never had a party in all my life, would it be too much to celebrate by having one?' and she said, 'Not at all, though I should first like to know what girls you would like to invite,' and I told her all the G. R. Club. 'Anyone else?' she asked, and I thought of Nettie Black. 'I'd like to have Nettie,' I said, and then I remembered how lonely I used to be even at the Friendless, and how glad I used to be when you came to see me, Edna, and I thought of two or three who were still there, girls who haven't been adopted, and I said I'd like to have them. Then mother said, 'Very well, only the others may not want to come if you have poor children like them, and you'd better ask the girls, and if they refuse you can make up your mind which you would rather have, the girls of the club or the Friendlessers.'"

"Oh, Margaret, you know we won't care," said Edna earnestly.

"I knew *you* wouldn't, but I didn't know about them all. I shall have to ask, you see, because it seems to me that of all the people I know, the Friendlessers are the very ones who ought to come when it is to celebrate my coming away from there, and then, too they don't have good times like we do."

The girls all called the Home of the Friendless "The Friendless" and the children there, "The Friendlessers" so they knew quite well whom Margaret meant.

"How soon is the party to be?" asked Jennie.

"Next Saturday afternoon. The Friendlessers can come then better than any other time, and besides we live out of town, and it will be easier for everyone to come in the afternoon."

"I shall come," said Dorothy decidedly, "and I think it is a beautiful idea for you to have the Friendlessers."

"And of course I shall come," put in Jennie.

"I know my sister will," said Edna.

"And mine," echoed Dorothy.

"There is one thing I hope you won't mind my saying," said Margaret; "mother says please not to wear party frocks, and not to dress up much, on account of the Friendlessers, you know, for of course they won't have any."

"Of course not," agreed the girls.

"Mother says we can have just as good a time if we are not dressed up and as long as it is going to be in the daytime it won't make so much difference."

"Let's go tell the other girls," suggested Edna.

They hunted up Agnes, Celia and the rest of the club members and did not find one who objected to the presence of the "Friendlessers."

However, when the news of Margaret's party was noised abroad, there was much scorn on the part of the Neighborhood Club. "The idea," said Clara, "of going to a party with orphan asylum children! I'd like to see my mother allowing me to associate with such creatures. I can't think what Jennie Ramsey's mother can be thinking of to allow her to go. Besides, Margaret is an orphan asylum girl herself and no better than the rest! I'm sure I wouldn't be seen at her party."

"And they're not even going to wear party frocks, nor so much as white ones," said Gertrude Crane. "I don't see what fun it will be."

"And I suppose there are to be no boys," put in Clara.

"I haven't heard whether there are to be or not," returned Gertrude.

The question of boys did come up later when Mrs. MacDonald asked Margaret if she did not think it would be well to invite Frank and Charley Conway, as one of the "Friendlessers" was a boy. The two Porter boys who came out often to play with the Conway boys, were thought of and were invited, and when Edna returned home on Friday evening Cousin Ben informed her that he, too, was going.

"Why, Cousin Ben," she said in pleased surprise, "how does that happen, when you are such a big boy, really a man, you know?"

"I must confess I fished for an invitation," he told her. "Mrs. MacDonald was over here to ask if Charlie and Frank could come and I said, 'What's the matter with asking me, too?' and so I got my invite. I wouldn't miss it for a six-pence." Cousin Ben and Mrs. MacDonald were great friends and he was quite intimate at the big gray house so it was no wonder that he wanted to be at Margaret's first party.

It was as Ben said "a queer mix-up." The first to arrive were the four children from the Home of the Friendless, three little girls and one little boy. One of the teachers brought them out and remained in order to take them back again. The big gray house looked cheerful and more attractive than usual, for flowers were Mrs. MacDonald's great pleasure and they were everywhere, making up for the plainness of the furnishings, for Mrs. MacDonald did not believe in showiness. Her house was thoroughly comfortable but not elegant.

These first arrivals were very shy, quite awe-stricken and sat on the edges of their chairs scarce daring to move until Margaret took them out to see the greenhouses. After that they were a little more at their ease for each came back with a flower. By a little after three all had arrived, the Porter boys with their Punch and Judy show which they had promised to bring, and Ben with his banjo. All the girls wore plain frocks with no extra ornaments, Margaret herself being not much better dressed than her friends from the Home.

The Punch and Judy show was given first as a sort of prelude to the games which were to follow, and in these even the older girls joined with spirit. The main idea seemed to be that everyone should do his or her best to make the party a success and to give the poorer children as good a time as possible. Ben, be it said, was the life of the occasion. He kept everyone going, never allowed a dull moment, and if nothing else was planned, he would pick up his banjo and give a funny coon song, so that it was no wonder Mrs. MacDonald was glad to have invited him.

Probably in all their lives the Friendlessers never forgot the wonderful table to which they were led when refreshments were served, and which they talked of for weeks afterward. Here there was no stint and the decorations were made as beautiful as possible. There were pretty little favors for everyone, and such good things to eat as would have done credit to any entertainment. It was all over at six o'clock, but not one went away with a feeling of having had a stupid time, for even the older girls agreed among themselves that it had been great fun.

"Did you ever see anything like those children's eyes when they saw that table," said Agnes smiling at the recollection.

"It must have been like a fairy tale to them, poor little things," replied Helen Darby. "I think it was a perfectly lovely thing for Mrs. MacDonald to do. Won't I have fun telling father about it, and how interested he will be. He has been quizzing me all day about my orphan asylum party, but I know he liked my going."

"I liked that little Nettie Black," Florence remarked. "She has such a nice quaint little face, like an old-fashioned picture. Her name ought to be Prudence or Charity or some of those queer old names. Where did you pick her up, Edna?"

"Oh, she is the little girl that I kept house with at the time of the blizzard," Edna told her. "She lives just a short way up the side road, and she is a very nice child."

"I found that out," returned Florence. "Why doesn't she belong to our club?"

"Because she doesn't go to our school."

"To be sure, I forgot that. Well, she could be made an honorary member or something, couldn't she Agnes?"

"Why, I should think so. We'll have to bring that up at our next meeting. Would she like to belong to the club, do you think, Edna?"

"She would just love to, I know."

"Then we'll have to fix it some way. I'll ask mother or Mrs. Conway what we can do."

"I don't know how we could all get into their parlor," said Edna doubtfully; "it is so very tiny."

"We don't have to," Agnes told her, "for you know the general club-room is up in our attic and I'm sure that is big enough for anyone. If Nettie comes into the club, when her turn comes for a meeting it can be held in the general club-room."

This was very satisfactory, but it did not do away with another difficulty which came to Edna's mind. She knew that Mrs. Black had barely enough means to get along on with the utmost economy and how Nettie could ever furnish even simplerefreshments for a dozen or more girls she did not know. However, she would not worry about that till the time came. As yet Nettie was not even a member of the club.

Margaret's party was talked about at school almost as much after as before it came off. Those who had been present discoursed upon the good time they had had, and those who were not there wished they had been. But to offset it, there came the report that Clara Adams was going to have a party and that it would be in the evening and was expected to be a gorgeous affair. Jennie Ramsey was invited but had not made up her mind whether she wanted to go or not. As most of those who would be invited were the children of Mrs. Adams's friends and were not schoolmates of Clara's it did not seem to Jennie that she would have a very good time.

"It will be all fuss and feathers," she told Dorothy and Edna, "and I won't know half the children there, besides I shall hear so much talk about what I shall wear and all that, I believe I'd rather stay at home."

"Clara is going to wear a lace frock over pink silk, I heard her say," Dorothy told them.

"I should think that would be very pretty," declared Edna admiringly.

"I'd rather be dressed as we were at Margaret's," Jennie returned, "for then we could romp around and not care anything about what happened to our clothes." Jennie hadn't a spark of vanity and cared so little for dress as to be a surprise to the others.

"Of course that was nice, but I should like the pretty clothes, too," rejoined Edna with honesty.

"They won't do anything, either, but dance and sit around and look at each other," continued Jennie. "I'd much rather play games like 'Going to Jerusalem' and 'Forfeits' and all those things we did at Margaret's. I have all the dancing I want at dancing-school. No, I shall tell my mother I don't want to go." Jennie had made up her mind, and that was the end of the matter for her.

Therefore the others heard very little of what went on at Clara's party. That it came off they knew, and there was much talk of what this one or that one wore, of how late they stayed and how many dances they had, but that was all, and the stay-at-homes decided that, after all they had not missed much, and if Clara's intention was to rouse their envy she failed of her purpose.

At the next meeting of the club Nettie was voted in as an honorary member. "That seems to be about the only thing we can do," Agnes announced, "and everyone seems to want her." So the thing was done.

If there was one thing above another which Nettie did long for it was to become a member of the club whose wonderful doings she had heard so much of from Edna. The two had seen each other often, and now that the spring was nearing, rarely a Saturday came but that they met. It was Edna who took her the joyful news on Friday evening.

"I've something perfectly lovely to tell you," she announced as soon as she was inside the door of the little house.

"What?" asked Nettie with a quick smile of interest.

"You're going to be a member of our club."

"Oh, Edna, how can I be? I don't go to your school."

"I know, and that is why we had to make you an honorary member," Agnes said.

"Oh, I think you are all the dearest things I ever knew," cried Nettie. Then her face fell, "But, oh, Edna, how can we get all of you girls in this little bit of a house?"

"Oh, you can meet in the general club-room at the Evanses," Edna told her. "Agnes says so and it is in their attic, you know. When a girl can't very well have the meeting at her house we have it there. Once it was to be at Betty Lowndes's house and her little sister had the chicken-pox so we couldn't meet there and we had it in the attic."

Nettie's face cleared, but presently a new difficulty presented itself, one which she hesitated to speak of but which was a very serious one. How should she tell Edna what was in her mind? But she remembered that Edna had seen the poverty of the family stores and that there was no need to make any pretence to her. "There's another thing," she began, "I haven't any money, and I couldn't ask mother for refreshments."

"I thought of that," answered Edna; "we might give them rice," and then they both laughed. "If there were only some way you could earn some money and I could help you," continued Edna with more seriousness. "Perhaps we could think of some way. If it were something we could both do, I could help you."

"You are always so good that way," replied Nettie gratefully.

"Well, anyhow," said Edna, "it won't be for some time yet that you have to have the meeting and perhaps we can think of something. If we can't would you mind if I ask mother what we could do?"

"I'd rather not," replied Nettie doubtfully, "not unless you have to."

"Then I won't unless I have to."

"Perhaps my mother can think of a way, only I don't want to say anything to her, for she will feel badly because she can't let me have the money, and I know I ought not to ask her for it. I won't ask, of course, but if I tell it will be the same as asking, and it will make her feel so unhappy if she must say no, she can't."

"Then we must try very hard to think of a way without telling anyone. You wouldn't need so very much, you know, Nettie, for we can have real cheap things like peanuts and gingerbread, or something like that. I believe fifty cents would be enough to spend, and a dollar would be plenty."

This seemed like a large amount to Nettie, though she did not say so, and the thought of earning that much weighed heavily upon her after Edna had gone home.

Edna's thoughts, too, were busy all the evening, and she was so absorbed in Nettie's dilemma that she sat with arms on the table and doing nothing but looking off into space so that at last her father said. "What's the matter, little girl? You haven't even asked for your favorite children's page of my evening paper," and he handed it over to her.

This was something that Edna always asked for and she took it now with some little interest, and roused herself to look down the columns. Presently she breathed softly. "Oh!" She had seen something which gave her an idea for Nettie, and she went to bed that night full of a hope which she meant her friend should know as soon as possible the next day.

CHAPTER IX

THE PUZZLE

When Edna awoke on Saturday morning her first thought was of Nettie and she scrambled out of bed that she might not lose a moment's time in telling her of the discovery she had made the night before. She hurried through her breakfast and was off to the little house as soon as she had been given leave by her mother. She carried the page of her father's paper safely folded in her hand, and ran nearly all the way, arriving breathless. She could scarcely wait for Nettie to open to her knock, and her words tumbled over each other as she replied to Nettie's greeting of "How nice and early you are," by saying, "Oh, I have something so nice to tell you."

"You had something nice to tell me when you came last evening," returned Nettie; "you don't mean to say there is anything more."

"Yes, I've found a way that maybe you can make some money, a dollar."

This was exciting, "Oh, do tell me quick," returned Nettie.

Edna hastily began to open the paper she carried, and then she thrust it before Nettie, pointing to a line and saying, "There, read that."

Nettie did as she was told, her eyes eagerly running over the words. "Oh, Edna," she said, "do you believe we could do it?"

"Why, of course, but you see the main thing is to get it done as quickly as possible, for the one who gets the answer to the puzzle the quickest and who has the clearest answer will get the first prize. Maybe we couldn't get the very first, but we could get the second, and that's a dollar. We must set to work right away. I thought we'd do the best we could and then we'd get Cousin Ben to fix it up for us."

"Would that be right?"

"Oh, I think so, for it doesn't say you mustn't have any help; it just says the one who sends it in the soonest. I left a note for Cousin Ben to stop here if he had time this morning."

"Do you think he will?"

"If he has time. I told him it was something very particular. You don't mind his knowing, do you, Nettie? He won't tell, I am sure. You don't know how well he can keep a secret."

60

"No, I don't mind," Nettie replied, "because he has been here and knows all about everything."

"Then let's go at it."

"I must finish the dishes first."

"Then would you rather I should help you with them or start on the puzzle?"

"I think you'd better start on the puzzle."

"Very well. I've been thinking a little about it, and I believe I've guessed part. They are in the paper every week on Fridays, and I often do them, but this is the first time I've noticed that a prize has been offered."

She took off her coat and hat, sat down at the table and spread out the paper before her. Nettie furnished paper and pencil and then went back to her work in the kitchen. The two were busying their brains over the puzzle when Ben appeared an hour later.

"Hallo," he said, "what's up, kiddies?"

"Why you see," Edna began, "Nettie has been taken into the club, and when her time comes to have the club meeting she won't have any way of getting the refreshments, so we thought and thought of what we could do to get some money, and last night I saw in the Children's Corner of the *Times* that they would give prizes for guessing a puzzle, you know those puzzles, Cousin Ben."

"Yes, my child, I knew them of yore."

"Well, don't you see if we can only guess this one quick and can send in the answer right away we might get a dollar, anyhow. We have guessed a lot of it, but I thought maybe you could help us a little and tell us how to fix it up very nicely. Have you very much to do to-day?"

"Not so much but that I can spare you a little time for such laudable ambition. Where's your puzzle?"

Edna produced the paper and then showed him what they had already done. "Do you think it is right as far as we've gone?" she asked anxiously.

He looked over the page she offered him. "Pretty good so far. Let me see. I think that must be John B. J on B. you see."

"Of course, it is, why didn't we think of that? And this one, what do you think that can be?"

Ben looked at this thoughtfully, and presently declared he had it. So bit by bit the puzzle was completed and within an hour was in such shape as pleased the girls immensely.

"Now," said Ben, "I'll tell you what I can do. I want to take the noon train to town and I'll get this right down to the newspaper office myself; I have to go near there, and so it will reach them much quicker than if it were sent by mail, you see."

"Oh, Cousin Ben, you are a perfect dear!" cried Edna. "I think that is just lovely of you. We are so much obliged, aren't we, Nettie?"

"I am very much obliged to both of you," returned Nettie sedately. Edna's interest was so great that she forgot she was not doing this for herself at all.

"Shall we tell your mother?" asked Edna when Ben had gone, promising that he would attend to the puzzle the very first thing.

"Why—" Nettie hesitated, "I'd like to have her know and yet I would love dearly to have it for a surprise if we did win. When do you suppose we will know?"

"Not before next Friday, I suppose, but that will be soon enough, won't it?"

"Yes, except that I can scarcely wait to know, and it is hard to keep a secret from your mother that long."

"Why don't you tell her that you have a secret and that you can't tell her till Friday?"

"I might do that, but then suppose I shouldn't win; we would both be disappointed."

"What did you tell her just now that we were all doing?"

"I told her we were doing a puzzle, and she said as long as I had done my morning's work I could stay with you. I have still my stockings to darn, but I can do those this afternoon. Mother always lets me do them when I choose; so long as I get them done before Sunday, that is all she asks."

Edna looked very sympathetic. She did not have to do her stockings nowadays, though she remembered that it had been one of the week's tasks when she was staying with Aunt Elizabeth, and it was one she much disliked. She stayed a little while longer and then returned home, for Dorothy was coming that afternoon and they were both going over to see Margaret to make what Dorothy said was their party call.

The weather was quite mild; already the buds were beginning to swell on the trees, and the crocuses were starting up in the little grass plot in front of Nettie's home. Edna stopped to look at them as she passed out. She was full of Nettie's secret but she had promised not to tell. She wished Cousin Ben would come back so she could talk it over with him, but he was not to return till late in the day and meantime she must occupy herself and not say a word of what was uppermost in her mind.

She found Celia and Agnes in the library talking earnestly. There was a pleasant aroma of gingerbread pervading the house, and the fire in the open grate looked very cheerful. What a dear place home was, and how glad she was always to get back to it. Agnes held out her hand as she came in. "Well, chickabiddy," she said, "where have you been? You are as rosy as an apple."

"I've been down to Nettie's. I'm glad I don't have to darn my stockings."

"Does Nettie have to?"

"Yes, and she has to wash the dishes, too. I did darn my stockings last year, but Katie does them all this year, so I don't even have to be sorry for mother and think of her doing them, for Katie is paid to do them."

Agnes laughed. "But I have no doubt you would do them just as cheerfully as Nettie does, if you had to do them."

"I don't know about the cheerful part, but I wouldn't yell and scream."

"Let us hope you would not," said Celia. "I should hope you knew better than to behave like that."

"Of course," said Edna. "What were you talking about, you two?"

"Shall we tell her, Agnes?" asked Celia.

"Why not? It will soon be talked over by all of us."

"Well, we were talking of having something very special for the last meeting of the club, after school closes. You see most of the girls go away for the summer, and we shall have to give the club a holiday, too."

"What nice special thing were you thinking of?"

"We thought if we could have some nice little fairy play and have it out of doors, it would be lovely. We would invite our parents and the teachers and have a real big affair."

"How perfectly lovely. What is the play?"

"Oh, dear, we haven't come to that yet. We did think some of having 'Alice in Wonderland,' but that has been done so often. We were wishing for something original."

"Why don't you get Cousin Ben to help you? He has so many funny things to say about the woodsy creatures."

"The very one. Why didn't we think of him before, Agnes? He may be silly about some things, but he would certainly have ideas about that. Where is he, Edna?"

"He has gone in town, and won't be back till late in the afternoon."

"Trust you for keeping track of his movements," said Celia laughing. "I don't believe Ben yawns but Edna knows it. Well, we will see what he says this evening."

"Couldn't you and he come to our house after supper?" asked Agnes.

"I'll find out and 'phone you when he comes in. He doesn't generally have anything special on hand Saturdays, unless something is going on at the Abercrombies'."

This gave Edna a new theme to think of and in consequence she did not find it hard to keep from talking of Nettie's secret when she and Dorothy met that afternoon.

They took the news of the probable play to Margaret who wanted at once to tell Mrs. MacDonald about it. She showed great interest and asked all sorts of questions. "Why couldn't you have it here in my grounds?" she asked. "There is a good place just back of the house where the terrace is. I hope you will let it be Margaret's meeting and let me furnish everything."

"Oh, Mrs. Mac, there will be ever and ever so many people, for we are going to ask our families and the teachers and all those." Edna was quite overpowered.

"Well, what of that? Haven't I as much right to entertain them as any of the others have, and have I less room than my neighbors?"

"Why, no, you have more."

"Very well, then. I put in my plea the first one and I hope you will lay it before your next meeting." She spoke almost as if she were angry but there was a merry little twinkle in her eyes which the girls had come to know well. The next words were, "Go out, Margaret, and ask Lizzie to send in some of the day's baking for your friends. There must be scones, or something of that kind." The girls liked the Scotchy things, as they called them, that Mrs. MacDonald had for them, and the hot scones, with a "wee bittie" of honey or jam were generally as pleasant a treat as they found anywhere.

When Edna had returned from her visit she told Celia of what Mrs. MacDonald had offered and before they had finished talking of it, Cousin Ben came in, and was immediately set upon, though Edna ran out to meet him in the hall that she might whisper, "Did you leave it all right?"

"First thing," he returned. "It couldn't have been an hour from the time I left you before it was at the office."

"Oh, goody, goody!" exclaimed Edna softly, patting her hands together. "Agnes has been here, Cousin Ben, and Celia wants to ask you something. Come into the library, please."

He followed her in and the subject was opened to him of the little fairy play.

He shook his head. "Can't promise. That's a good deal to spring on a fellow unbeknownst. I'll have to think about it."

"But can't you go over to Agnes's this evening to talk it over?" asked Celia.

Now Ben admired Agnes very much, though he would not have it known for the world. "I was going to Abercrombies," he said with apparent reluctance.

"Oh, but you see Will Abercrombie every day," said Celia coaxingly, "and we do so want to have your help, Ben."

"Well, perhaps I can 'phone to Will not to expect me," said Ben giving in. "But if I take hold of this thing you girls will all have to do your part."

"Oh, we will," Celia promised earnestly. "We are none of us up to an original play, but you are."

"Such flattery," laughed Ben. "Well, if I am going to call on ladies I must go up and make myself look respectable."

"He'll do it," said Celia, as soon as her cousin had left the room. "He has as good as promised."

Whatever was said that evening was not reported, but it is enough to say that Ben had promised to see what he could do, and would let them know later when he had gone over the subject more thoroughly, so with this the girls had to be satisfied.

There was no more to be heard of either puzzle or play during the week while school was occupying them all, but on Friday Mrs. MacDonald's offer was presented to the club and unanimously accepted with thanks.

There was no delay in Edna's demand for the evening paper on that Friday, but to her great disappointment her father found that he had left it in the car, and there was no way to get another copy till the next day. Edna was almost in tears, for she had so counted on letting Nettie know the very first thing in the morning.

"I am so sorry," said her father. "I forgot entirely that the Friday issue was the one in which you are always so interested. I will bring you out a copy to-morrow, daughter. I will try not to forget it, but I give you leave to call me up on the long distance, or rather the out-of-town line and get you to remind me. If you will call, say, at about ten o'clock, I will send one of the boys out for it from the office."

This was certainly more than Edna had any right to expect, and she thanked him as heartily as she could, though deep down in her heart the disappointment still lingered and she felt that it would be harder still for Nettie to wait another day.

However, she went early to the little house as she had promised, and saw Nettie at the window on the watch for her. She looked so pleased when she saw her friend that Edna was all the more grieved at having to tell her she must wait till evening. "Oh, I am so glad you have come," cried Nettie as she met her at the door. "I have been watching for you for ages." And she drew her inside.

CHAPTER X

A DOWNFALL OF PRIDE

"Oh, Edna, Edna!" Nettie jumped up and down and fairly hugged her friend in her joy.

"Why, why," Edna began, but Nettie interrupted her with "I have it! I have it!"

"Have what?" Edna was still mystified.

"The prize! The prize! I won it. The money came in the mail this morning."

Edna had not counted on this possibility and it was as much of a surprise to her as it had been to Nettie. "Oh! Oh! Oh!" she cried, and she, too, began to dance up and down hugging Nettie as fervently as Nettie had hugged her. "Have you told your mother?"

"Oh, yes, I couldn't possibly keep it."

"Do show me what they said." So Nettie took her in and showed her the precious letter with the enclosed order for a dollar, which made it seem a very real thing.

"Ben will be so pleased," said Edna with satisfaction. "It is really owing to him that it got there soon enough."

"And to you for helping me and for telling me in the first place. I think I ought to divide with you."

"Why, Nettie Black, you won't do any such thing. Don't you know that it was all on your account that we did it in the first place?"

"Ye-es, but after your doing so much it doesn't seem fair for you to have none of it."

"I'll have some of the refreshments, won't I?"

Nettie laughed. "I hope so."

"Have you decided what you will have?"

"Not exactly. I thought I would wait till you came to talk it over with mother. You said something about gingerbread and my mother can make the nicest you ever saw."

"Would she make some for you? I wonder if it would cost very much. None of the girls have had gingerbread, and I am sure it would be liked."

"Then let's go see what mother says."

Mrs. Black was in the kitchen making bread for her Saturday baking. She smiled on the two children's eager faces which showed that something of unusual interest was going on. "Mother," began Nettie, "you know I am to have the club meeting after a while, and it is to be at the general club-room at Miss Agnes Evans's house, and you know we always have refreshments," Nettie spoke as if she had already attended every meeting, when that of the afternoon before had been her very first.

"Yes, I remember you told me, dear," said her mother.

"And I told you that was why we tried for the puzzle prize, so that I could pay for my refreshments. Does gingerbread cost very much?"

"No, my dear, it costs less than any other kind of cake."

"But how much? I mean how much would it cost to make enough for—for fourteen girls?"

"Why, not a great deal. I could bake them in the little scalloped pans so they would be more crusty. I don't believe it would cost more than twenty-five cents, for you know we have our own eggs."

"Good! Then what else could I have? We can't have more than three things."

"Let me think for a minute and I will perhaps be able to suggest something." She went on kneading her bread while the children watched her. Presently she said: "I have a bottle of raspberry shrub that your Aunt Henrietta gave me and which we have never used. Would you like to have that? I can recommend it as a very nice drink, and I should be very glad to donate it."

"Would it be nice?" Nettie looked at Edna for endorsement.

"I think it would be perfectly delicious," she decided, "and nobody has had anything like that. We have had ginger ale and lemonade, and chocolate and such things."

"Then, mother, that will be very nice, thank you," said Nettie, as if Edna were at the other end of a telephone wire. "Now for number three. I shall have ever so much to spend on that, so I could have most anything."

"What have the other girls had?" Mrs. Black asked Edna.

"Oh, different things. Some have had sandwiches and chocolate and some kind of candy, and some have had ice cream and cake and candy; some have had—let me see—cake and lemonade and fruit, but the third thing is generally some kind of candy."

"Do you remember what Uncle David sent us last week?" Mrs. Black asked Nettie.

"The maple sugar? Oh, yes, but would it be nice to have just little chunks of maple sugar?"

"No, but don't you know what delicious creamy candies we made by boiling and stirring it? Why not do some of it that way? It would be a little out of the usual run, and quite unlike what is bought at the shops."

"What do you think, Edna?" Nettie again appealed to her friend.

"I think it would be fine. Oh, Nettie you will have things that aren't a bit like anyone else has had and they will all be so good. I am sure the girls will say so."

Nettie beamed. This was such a pleasant thing to hear. "But I haven't spent but twenty-five cents of my prize money," she said.

"Are you so very sorry for that?" her mother asked.

"No, but—Is it all mine, mother, to do what I choose with, even if I don't spend it for the club?"

"Why, of course, my dear. You earned it, and if I am able to help you out a little that should make no difference."

"Then I think I know what I should like to do with it. I shall make two secrets of it and one I shall tell you, mother, and the other I can tell Edna."

"Tell me mine now," said Edna getting down from the chair.

Nettie took her off into the next room where there was much whispering for the next few minutes. "I shall get something for mother," Nettie explained. "I don't know exactly what but I will find out what she needs the most."

"I think that is a perfectly lovely plan," agreed Edna. "Now I must go back and tell Ben, for he will want to know. You come up this afternoon, Nettie, won't you?"

Nettie promised, and after Edna had gone she said to her mother, "Mother, I think I will spend part of my money on a birthday gift for Edna. It was all her

69

doings about the puzzle and I would like to have her have something I could buy with the money. Will you help me?"

"Indeed I will, my dear, and I think that is an excellent plan."

So Nettie had her two secrets and in time both gifts were given.

Her meeting was an interesting one. The girls always liked the old attic and it was seldom that a meeting there did not turn out to be one which was thoroughly enjoyed. The refreshments received even more praise than Edna had predicted, for not a crumb of gingerbread, not a single maple-sugar cream, nor a drop of raspberry shrub was left, and the honorary member went home in an exalted frame of mind.

On the very evening of this meeting, while Edna was looking over her favorite page of her father's paper, she heard him say to his wife. "Humph. That was a bad failure of Green and Adams to-day. Adams was a pretty high-flyer, and a good many of the men on the 'Change have been prophesying this crash."

"What Adams is that?" asked Mrs. Conway.

"Oliver Adams. He lives on the square, you know, in that large white house with the lions in front."

Edna pricked up her ears. "Is it Clara Adams's father?" she asked.

"Does she live on the square?" asked her mother.

"Yes, in a big white house with lions in front just like father said."

"Then, of course, it is the same."

"What has happened to him, mother?"

"He has lost a great deal of money, dear?"

"Oh, poor Clara."

"I'm afraid she will be poor Clara sure enough," returned her father. "He can't keep up that way of living very long. His wife is as extravagant as he is, and I doubt if there is much left out of the estate."

Edna wondered if Clara would have to live in a tiny, little house like Nettie's and if she would be very unhappy. Would she leave school, and—There were so many wonderings that she asked her mother a great many questions, and went off on Monday morning feeling quite ready to give Clara all the sympathy she needed.

But Clara was not at school on Monday, but on the next day she appeared. The news of her father's failure was common talk so that every girl in school had heard of it, and wondered if it would have any effect on Clara. For a time it did not, but in a short time it was whispered about that the Adamses had removed to another street and into a much smaller house. Clara no longer came to school in the automobile, and those girls who had clung to her on account of the powers of riches now openly deserted, declared that she had left their neighborhood and in consequence could no longer belong to their club. Then in a little while it was announced that the club had disbanded, and the remaining members came in a body and begged that they might be taken into the G. R.'s. There was much discussion. Some were for, some were against it, but finally the rule of the club was acted upon and the five new members took their places, leaving Clara in lonely grandeur. She treated this desertion with such open scorn and was so very unpleasant to those who had formerly been her friends, that they turned their backs upon her utterly, declaring that they would rather pay a fine every day in the week than be nice to Clara Adams.

"Hateful thing!" Edna heard Nellie Haskell say one day quite loud enough for Clara to hear. "She's kept us out of a lot of fun and we were geese to keep in with her so long. I'm sorry I ever had anything to do with her. I think she is the most disagreeable girl that ever was."

Edna looked over at Clara who was sitting very still by herself on a bench in one corner of the playground. She looked after the three girls who had just passed and were now walking down the path with their arms around one another. So had she seen them with Clara not so very long before. She thought she would go over and say something to her old enemy, but what to say—She had no good excuse. Then she remembered an exceedingly pretty paper-doll which had been sent her by her Cousin Louis Morrison. His aunt had painted it and it was much handsomer than one ordinarily saw. Edna had it in the book she carried. She drew in her breath quickly, then started over to Clara's corner.

"Don't you want to see my paper-doll?" she asked. "It is such a beauty." And without waiting for an answer she opened her book and held out the doll for Clara to see. It was given rather a grudging glance, but it was really too pretty not to be admired and Clara replied with a show of indifference, "It is quite pretty, isn't it?"

Edna sat down by her. "I will show you some of her dresses," she went on. Clara loved paper-dolls, and she could not but be a little interested. Anything which was painted or drawn was of more interest to her than most things. She had shown her talent in that way by the fatal caricature.

"Somebody told me you could make mighty pretty paper-dolls," Edna went on, bound to make herself agreeable.

"I do make them sometimes," replied Clara a little more graciously, "but I could never make any as pretty as this. I can copy things pretty well, but I can't make them up myself."

For a moment Edna struggled with herself. The doll was a new and very precious possession, but—She hesitated only a moment and then she said: "Would you like to copy this? I will lend it to you if you would like to."

There was a time when Clara might have spurned even this kind offer, setting it down as "trying to get in" with her, but her pride and vanity had received a blow when the Neighborhood Club was broken up and she cast forth, and she took the offer in the spirit in which it was meant. "Oh, would you do that?" she said. "I should love to copy it and I will take awfully good care of the doll."

"You can take it now," said Edna laying the doll on the other's lap. There should be no chance for her to change her mind. Clara slipped the doll into one of her books and just then the bell rang, so they went in together.

After school Dorothy clutched her chum. "Edna Conway," she cried, "did I see you talking to Clara Adams?"

"Um-huh," returned Edna.

"Well, you are the greatest one. I should think after all she has done that you would want to keep as far away from her as possible."

"Well," said Edna. "I said I was going to be nice to her if ever I had the chance and I had the chance."

"If you are going with her, I can tell you that all the girls will turn their backs on you."

"I didn't say I was going with her all the time, but I don't see why I can't speak to her if I want to."

"Oh, I suppose you can speak, but I shouldn't do much more than that."

Edna made no reply. She had her own ideas of what she meant to do.

"Where is your paper-doll?" asked Dorothy, "I want to show it to Agnes."

"I haven't it with me," returned Edna a little confusedly.

"You had it when we went down to recess. Is it in your desk? Go on and get it, that is a dear. Agnes wants to see it."

"It isn't in my desk. I haven't it," returned Edna bluntly.

72

"You don't mean to say you have given it away? Edna Conway, you can't have given it to Clara Adams!" Dorothy's voice expressed horror and dismay.

"No, I haven't *given* it to her; I only lent it to her," replied Edna.

"Well, of all things!" Dorothy was stricken dumb for a moment. Then she put her arms around her friend and hugged her. "You are an angel," she said. "I couldn't have done such a thing to save me, and I don't believe there is another girl in the school who could. I'm going to tell Agnes."

"Oh, please don't," begged Edna.

But Dorothy was off and presently Agnes came over to where the two had been standing. "What did you lend Clara your doll for, Edna?" she asked.

"Because I didn't want to pay a fine," replied she.

Agnes laughed. "That is one way out of it. I suppose the next thing we know you will be proposing that we ask Clara Adams into our club. Half the girls will leave if you do, I can promise you that."

This was something very like a threat, and it had the effect Agnes meant it should, though it did not prevent Edna from making plans of her own concerning Clara. She smiled at her as she took her seat in class the next morning, and for the very first time in all her life she received from Clara a smile in return.

73

CHAPTER XI

A NEW MEMBER

During this time Miss Newman had not won more than respect from her girls. She was an excellent teacher and kept good order, but she had too severe a manner to call forth affection. Nevertheless she did appreciate any little kindness done her, and was not unwilling to repay when the opportunity came. Dorothy and Edna had always stood up for her, and had brought her the small gifts which children like to take their teachers, a particularly large and rosy apple, a bunch of flowers, a more important present at Christmas and a growing plant at Easter. They did not know much about her home life, for she was not the affable person Miss Ashurst had been. Uncle Justus had told Edna that she lived with an invalid sister in quite a different quarter of the city, and that she had a long way to come to school.

One spring afternoon as Celia and Edna were starting forth, a sudden shower overtook them. They were going home every day now as they had done in the early fall, and were hurrying for their train when they saw Miss Newman just ahead of them without an umbrella. "There's Miss Newman," said Edna to her sister, "and she has no umbrella; I'm going to give her mine and come under yours, Celia," then before Celia could say a word she ran on ahead. "Please take my umbrella, Miss Newman," she said. "I can go under Celia's."

"But you may need it before Monday," said Miss Newman.

"Oh, no, I won't, for I am going straight home. We are to have a club meeting at the Evanses this afternoon, or I should not be in such a hurry."

"And I am in a hurry, too," said Miss Newman, "for I am very anxious to get home to my sister. Thank you very much for the umbrella. I should have had to go in somewhere, it is pouring so, and that would have delayed me."

By this time Celia came up and Edna slipped under her sister's umbrella. They took their car at the next corner, but they saw Miss Newman standing on the other side waiting for the car which should come along somewhat later. "Poor thing," said Edna as she looked from the car window; "she would have been soaked, Celia, if she had had to stand there without an umbrella, and she has a cold now."

Celia smiled. "I believe you would love a chimpanzee, or a snake, Edna."

"I think little green snakes are very pretty," returned Edna calmly. "Cousin Ben likes them, too. He showed me one in the grass last Sunday. I felt sorry for it because nearly everybody hates snakes, and Cousin Ben said this one was perfectly harmless."

"I draw the line at snakes," returned Celia. "I suppose you feel sorry for Miss Newman."

"Yes, I do; she is so unpretty."

Celia laughed. "That is a delicate way of putting it, I am sure. Well, I am glad she has one friend; no doubt she needs it. Most of the girls aren't so ready to say nice things of her as they were of Miss Ashurst."

"I know it," replied Edna, "and that is one reason Dorothy and I stand up for her. We say suppose we were as—as ugly as that, and had to go a long, long way to school every day to teach horrid girls who didn't be nice to us, how would we like it?"

"She looks like a cross old thing," returned Celia rather flippantly.

"She isn't exactly cross, but she isn't the kind you can lean up against and say 'what a pretty tie you have on,' as we did with Miss Ashurst. Celia, I am afraid Miss Newman never will get married."

Celia laughed. "Perhaps she doesn't want to. Everyone doesn't, you know."

This was rather beyond Edna's comprehension, and she sat pondering over the extraordinary statement till the car reached the station. She arrived early in the school-room on Monday morning to find Miss Newman already there. She looked up with a smile as the little girl entered. "I brought back your umbrella," she said. "I don't know what I should have done without it. I left my sister rather worse than usual and I wanted very much to get home as soon as possible."

"Is your sister ill?" asked Edna

"She is never very well. When she was a little girl, younger than you, she fell and hurt her spine. She has never been well since, and at times suffers very much."

"How was she this morning?" asked Edna sympathetically.

"She was much better. I left her sitting on the porch in the sun. She can walk only a few steps, you see, and sometimes has to be lifted from place to place."

"Who lifts her?" Edna was much interested at this peep into Miss Newman's life.

"I do when I am there, for I know just how to do it without hurting her."

"Will she sit there all day where you left her?"

75

"Oh, no, for she has a wheeling chair and the old woman who lives with us can wheel her in when she is ready to go."

"Tell me some more." Edna leaned her elbows on the table and looked at her teacher with a wistful look. She did feel so very sorry for this poor sister who could not walk.

"She is a very cheerful, bright person," Miss Newman went on, "and everyone loves her. She is very fond of children and is continually doing something for those in the neighborhood. It is far from being a wealthy street, and back of us there are many very poor people. At Christmas we had a tree for the ones who couldn't have one at home, and my sister made nearly everything on it, such pretty things they were, too. There was a present for each child."

"I think that was perfectly lovely," said Edna. This was the kind of thing that appealed to her. "What is your sister's name?"

"Her name is Eloise."

"I think that is a beautiful name. I should like very much to see her."

"She would like very much to see you, for she knows every one of my class, and asks about each one when I go home. You see she cannot go out into the world where I go, I have to take what I can of it to her." It was evident that this was the subject which was nearest to the teacher's heart, and that when talking of it she showed the gentlest side of her nature. "How would you like to go home with me this afternoon to see her, you and Dorothy Evans?"

"I would love to go, but are you sure she would like to have us come?"

"I don't know of anything that would please her more. She has never seen one of my pupils and has often longed to, for as I told you she has to see the world through my eyes, and anything that interests me interests her."

"I'll tell Dorothy as soon as she comes and I will ask Celia if I may go. Thank you, Miss Newman for inviting us." Then a number of girls came in and school was called to order before Edna had a chance to speak to her sister.

At recess, however, the matter was talked over, both Agnes and Celia listening attentively. "I don't think they ought to go home with Miss Newman," decided Agnes, "for she probably has dinner as soon as she gets home and it would make extra trouble. If they could go later it might be all right. I'd better go and talk to Miss Newman myself, then we can tell better what can be done." She went off and soon came back to say that she had arranged to go with the little girls later in the afternoon. "We can take a car from there which will connect with our line and in that way we shall not have to come all the way back into the city."

But a better arrangement than that was made, for when Margaret and Jennie heard of the affair they were so eager to be included in the party, that Miss Newman noticing their wistfulness, asked if they, too, would come. "There is nothing my sister likes better than to have a company of children around her to whom she can tell some tale. She is a great one for that, and often has as many as a dozen children on the porch," she told them.

"Then, I will tell you what we can do," said Jennie. "I know mother will say we may all go in the motor-car, and I can take you girls home just as well as not. I will call mother up now and tell her all about it." So in a few minutes the whole matter was arranged by telephone. The three little girls, Edna, Dorothy and Margaret were to go home with Jennie to luncheon and then they would make the start from there.

"That is just like the Ramseys," said Agnes, "they always come forward at just the right moment and do the thing that makes it pleasantest all around. Now we can go home at the usual time, Celia feeling perfectly safe about the girls."

Therefore about three o'clock on this bright afternoon in May they set forth in the automobile which was to take them to Miss Newman's and call for them later. Through a very unfamiliar part of the city they went till they came to a short street with a row of small houses on each side. Each house had a garden in front and a porch. In the very last one which had more ground around it than the rest, Miss Newman lived. The porch was covered with vines and in the garden there was a perfect wealth of flowers. A bird-cage in which a canary was singing, hung near the window. One end of the porch was screened by a bamboo shade. It was a very pretty nesty little place. Huddled down in a chair, with her head supported by pillows was Miss Eloise who smiled up at the girls as Miss Newman brought them forward one after another. Miss Eloise had a much more lovely face than her sister. Her eyes were beautiful, she had quantities of wavy dark hair, a sweet mouth and a delicate nose. The hand she held out was so small and fragile that when Edna clasped it in her plump fingers it seemed almost as if she were holding the claws of some bird.

"So this is Edna," she said. "She looks just as I thought she did. Dorothy I know her by her hair, and Margaret because she is the tallest of them, so of course the one left must be Jennie. I am so pleased to see you all. Sister, will you wheel me just a little further back so there will be more room for us all?"

Miss Newman was quick to spring to her sister's side, wheeling the chair at just the right angle, settling the pillows, and then passing her hand caressingly over Miss Eloise's dark locks. The girls could not imagine her so tender.

"I hope you are feeling well to-day," began Edna to start the conversation.

"Who wouldn't feel well in such glorious weather. It is such a beautiful world, and has so many interesting things in it. How is your sister, Edna?"

"She is very well," replied Edna, surprised that Miss Eloise should know she had a sister.

"And yours, Dorothy? I hear she is such a sweet, pretty girl."

Dorothy likewise surprised, made answer that Agnes was very well and would have come with them but that the four of them came in the Ramseys' motor-car.

"And wasn't it fun to see it come whirling up?" said Miss Eloise. "It was the very first time a motor-car ever came to our door, and I was excited over it. I think it was very sweet of Mrs. Ramsey to give me this pleasure, and, Margaret I cannot tell you how I enjoyed the flowers you used to bring to sister in the winter. Your mother must have the loveliest greenhouse. I never saw such fine big stalks of mignonette. We shall have mignonette a little later, for our flowers are coming on finely. As for the books you all gave sister at Christmas they have been a perfect feast. I am so glad to have you here and to be able to thank you for all the things you have done to make the long winter go more quickly for me."

The girls looked at one another. If they had known what their little gifts were to mean, how many times they could have added to them. They had not a word to say for they had not understood how a little ripple of kindness may widen till it touches an unknown shore.

"Now tell me about your club," Miss Eloise went on. "I should so like to hear what you did at the last meeting. Sister tells me all she can, but she doesn't have a chance to learn as much as I should like. I am so greedy, you see. I am like a child who says when you tell it a story, and think you have finished, 'Tell on.' I am always crying 'Tell on.' It is the most beautiful club I ever heard of and I am sorry I am not a little girl at your school so I could belong to it and enjoy the good times with you."

"But, darling, you have your own little club," said her sister, "and you are always thinking of what you can do for others."

"Oh, I know, but I live in such a tiny little world, and my 'little drops of water, little grains of sand' are such wee things."

"They mean a great deal more than you imagine," said her sister gently. "I am sure I could never live without them."

"Oh, that is because you make so much of me and what I do. She is a great sister," she said nodding to the girls. "She is a regular Atlas because she has to bring her world home on her back every day to me. Yes, indeed. Perhaps you don't think I am aware of all that goes on in that school-room. Why I even know when one of you misses a lesson, and if you will let me tell you a secret, I actually cried the day Clara Adams did the caricature."

"Oh, dear, oh, dear," Edna could not help sighing aloud while the other girls looked as much ashamed as if they had done the thing themselves. However, when Miss Eloise saw this she broke into a laugh and began to tell them of some very funny thing she had seen from the porch that morning, then followed one funny tale after another till the girls were all laughing till the tears ran down their cheeks. Miss Eloise had the drollest way of telling things, and the merriest laugh herself. After a while Miss Newman went inside and presently came out with a tray on which were glasses of lemonade and a plate of small cakes. These were passed around, and much enjoyed.

"Now tell them one of your stories," said Miss Newman to her sister.

"Shall I make up a new one or shall I tell them one of the old ones?"

"Tell them the one the Maginnis children like so much."

The children settled themselves in pleased anticipation, and a marvelous tale they listened to. Miss Eloise had a wonderful gift of story-telling and made every incident seem real and every character to stand out as vividly as if he or she were actually before them. The children listened in wrapt attention. She was a wonder to them.

The tale was scarcely over when up came the motor-car with Mrs. Ramsey in it. She stepped out and came in the gate and up to the porch. "I wanted to come, too, Miss Newman," she said. "I hope you don't mind."

"Oh, mother," cried Jennie, "you are just too late to hear the most beautiful story ever was."

"Now isn't that too bad?" said Mrs. Ramsey. "I feel guilty to interrupt this pleasant party, but I am afraid I shall have to take these girls home for it is getting late."

However, she did not hurry them and there was time for her to have a little talk with both Miss Newman and Miss Eloise. Just as she was about to take her leave she asked, "Do you think you would be able to take a little ride in the motor-car, Miss Eloise, if I were to come for you some day?"

"Oh, sister, could I?" Miss Eloise turned to Miss Newman, her eyes like stars. "I haven't been off this street for years," she said to Mrs. Ramsey.

"We would be very careful," said Mrs. Ramsey, seeing that Miss Newman looked doubtful. "The man could wheel the chair out to the car and could lift her in. It runs very smoothly and we would not go too fast nor on any of the streets which are not asphalt."

"Oh, sister!" Miss Eloise looked as pleadingly as any child.

"I have never wheeled her further than the corner," said Miss Newman, "for fear of the jolting when we had to go over the curb, but some day when she is feeling her best—"

"You will let me know—" put in Mrs. Ramsey eagerly. "Of course you will go, too, Miss Newman, and as soon as you think she has gone far enough we can come back. You know it is quite smooth and the riding easy going even as far as Brookside."

"Why that is our station," spoke up Edna.

Mrs. Ramsey nodded and smiled, and they said their good-bys leaving Miss Eloise feeling as if a new world were to open to her.

Of course Mrs. Ramsey listened to a full account of all that had gone on during the afternoon, and was deeply interested in the two sisters. "I just love Miss Newman," declared Dorothy. "She is the sweetest thing to her sister."

"They just adore one another," Jennie told her mother. "Miss Newman seems like some one else when I think of her now. I am so glad we went."

"So am I," replied her mother.

"And Miss Eloise knows all about our club and is so interested in it," Edna remarked. "Girls, we must always tell Miss Newman about the meetings after this so she can tell Miss Eloise all that goes on."

"Of course we must," they agreed.

"I know something better than that you could do," Mrs. Ramsey told them. "Why not make Miss Eloise an honorary member as you did Nettie Black? I think you could stretch your rule far enough not to make it out of the way to have one grown up person, when it is such a character as Miss Eloise. She could be the exception who will prove the rule."

"But, Mrs. Ramsey, she couldn't come to the meetings." Dorothy reminded her.

"No, but you could take turns in going to her; I mean you could appoint a committee of two to go to her each week and tell her about the previous meeting, then once in a while when she felt able, you could meet at her house."

"What a perfectly fine plan," cried Edna. "Will you tell Agnes and Celia about it, Mrs. Ramsey?"

"Why certainly, if you like."

"Now? This afternoon when you take us to our houses, Dorothy and me?"

"I don't see any objection."

The upshot of this was that Miss Eloise was admitted to the club to her intense delight. After Agnes and Celia had been to see her they were so enthusiastic that all the girls in the club by twos and threes paid her visits, and she came to know them every one.

CHAPTER XII

THE FLOWER PLAY

As the time approached for the flower play to be given attention there was considerable anxiety on the part of those who had taken it in hand. Ben declared that while he could do the main part of the work all right, he must have help of the girls in certain directions. "I'm no good at all when it comes to dialogue," he told them. "I can do the mechanical part, get the thing into shape for the stage, give you the general plot and all that, but you'll have to do the dialogue."

"Oh, but Ben," said Agnes, "suppose we can't."

"Then it will have to fall through."

The girls looked very sober over this; they realized that Ben was giving them more than they had any right to expect, and they could not ask him to give his studies second place. "Well," said Agnes rather dolefully, "we'll have to do the best we can."

"Angels can do no more," returned Ben, "and since you are so near to that class of beings you ought to be able to do something pretty fine."

The compliment had the effect of bringing a smile to Agnes's face and so the matter rested for that day. However, it was a subject which could not be allowed to rest for very long as the time was fast approaching when the parts must be given out for the girls to study. "And there will have to be ever so many rehearsals," said Agnes woefully to Celia as they were talking it over together on the Conways' porch.

"We don't seem to make a bit of headway," said Celia. "What we have written sounds so silly and flat. I'm afraid it will never be the kind of thing we hoped for."

"Ben has a lovely little plot and all the ideas he has given us about the scenes and the dressing of the characters and the funny situations are mighty good," returned Agnes, "it does seem as if between us all we ought to be able to do the rest when we have eighteen regular members in the club and two honorary ones."

Edna who was sitting on the top step listening attentively to all this, looked up. "Why don't you ask Miss Eloise to help you? She would love to, and she tells such beautiful, beautiful stories, you know."

"That is a brilliant idea," returned Agnes, "but she says she can never write them, she can only tell them."

"But couldn't she tell what to say and one of you write it down?"

Agnes looked at Celia and Celia looked at Agnes. "She has struck it, I do believe," cried Celia.

"Edna, honey, you are a child worth knowing," said Agnes. "The idea of your thinking of such a simple way out of the trouble when the rest of us were fumbling around for ideas. Of course that can be done, and as you say, I have no doubt but that Miss Eloise will be perfectly delighted to do anything she can for the club. Where is Ben? Do hunt him up, Edna, that's a good child."

As Edna generally knew Ben's haunts she was not long in finding him. He was much interested in what she had to say, threw down the book he was studying and went with her to join the girls. He was really very anxious to please them all and would go to almost any lengths to do it.

"Ben," cried Agnes as he came up on the porch. "Isn't that a fine scheme that Edna has thought of?"

"I should smile, and I have thought of just the stunt to get it in shape the quickest. If one of you girls will go with me to present me to the lady, I can take down what she says in shorthand and knock it off on the type-writer afterward. Then we'll all get together, you two girls, Miss Eloise and yours truly, and we'll put the whole thing into shape in double-quick time. How does that strike you?"

"Ben, you have saved our lives. When can you go to see Miss Eloise? This afternoon? It is Saturday and you haven't anything on hand more important than foot-ball, have you?"

"Do not speak slightingly of my athletic sports, if you please. However, I can forego the delights of being mauled for one afternoon, I reckon, and am at your service, fair lady. When shall you want to start?"

"Oh, right after luncheon, I think; as early as possible so as to have a good long afternoon. I do hope Miss Eloise is feeling fairly well to-day."

"Miss Newman says she is better all the time nowadays, since she has so much more to interest her," piped up Edna. "She told me yesterday that she had not had one of those dreadful attacks for ever so long."

"Then let us hope for the best," answered Ben.

It was exactly as Edna had predicted; Miss Eloise entered into the plan with the greatest eagerness, and when Ben had opened up his plot to her and had showed her how he had planned the scenes she said she would take a few minutes to think it over and then she thought she could give him some of the needed dialogue, and before they left Ben had taken down as much as was necessary for this first time, promising to come back for the rest.

"I'll get this into shape and bring it with me," he told Miss Eloise.

"And we can make copies so as to give out that much for the girls to learn," said Agnes.

They returned in high spirits, and for some time Ben's type-writing machine was heard clicking away. The characters had already been talked over and the principle ones given out. Ben had chosen very pretty fantastic names for the various flowers who were to be represented. Jennie was to be Pussy Willow; Edna, Pinky Blooms; Dorothy, Daisy White; Agnes, Rose Wild; Celia, Violet Blue, while Ben, himself was to be the old giant, Pine Knot, who lived in a swamp. It had been found necessary to introduce some of the boys into the play so Charlie and Frank Conway, Steve and Roger Porter were pressed into service. Charlie was to be Sassy Fras; Frank, Winter Green; Steve, Cran Berry, while Roger was to be the giant's henchman, Pine Needles.

The play was not to be for a week after school closed that they all might have plenty of time for its preparation without interfering with their school work. There was never very much fuss made over the closing by Uncle Justus, so there was not that excitement. Mr. Horner did not believe in showy commencements, and when the girls were graduated they simply received their diplomas after a few simple exercises, and then the school was dismissed. Therefore, the play was the great subject of conversation among the scholars. The girls who were already in the club were triumphantly sounding its praises to those who were not, while those who were not in were clamoring for entrance. However, it had been decided that no more new members would be admitted until fall, as there was already enough heart-burning over the players and their parts. The giving out of these had been left entirely to Miss Eloise who had chosen as she thought best, so there was at least no one of the girls to accuse of partiality. Margaret in the very beginning announced that her mother did not want her to take part and that she did not care to herself, as she was to have the fun of entertaining them all at her house, and moreover, she "couldn't act any more than a broomstick."

Of all the girls who felt the most bitter probably Clara Adams was the one who was chief among them. It was the greatest grievance she had ever known, in the first place not to take part in such a thing and in the second not even to be invited to the entertainment. Each girl in the club was allowed to ask two persons, and each one taking part in the play was allowed the same privilege, therefore, with her two brothers among the characters and her sister as well, Edna was free to ask anyone she chose. Mr. and Mrs. Horner had received an invitation from the whole club, so had Miss Newman, and the other teachers, and many of the pupils who were outside the charmed circle were invited by their schoolmates who were free to give invitations, only Clara Adams was not considered for a moment by anyone, and she was very miserable over the fact. If ever she regretted her past disagreeable treatment of her school fellows, it was now, but she would not have admitted this even to herself, although in her heart of hearts she was conscious of it being so.

"I'm not coming back here to school next year," she announced to Edna one day. The two had little chats once in a while and, to do Clara justice, she did her best to be pleasant whenever Edna gave her the chance.

"Oh, aren't you? Why not?" asked Edna.

Clara was silent for a moment, then she said, quite honestly, "My father can't afford to send me to such an expensive school. I suppose I shall have to go to the public school." Then in a new accession of pride, "Anyhow, father likes the public school better."

"Oh," Edna could not truthfully say she was sorry, for the fact, though she was sorry for the girl. She told the other girls what Clara had said and the gist of most of the responses was "Good riddance to bad rubbish." So it did not look very favorable for an enthusiastic farewell to poor Clara in the way of attentions to a departing friend. If anyone thought of her at all it was Edna, and she was too busy with all her other interests to give much regret to Clara.

It was only when her mother asked her one day, "Has anyone invited Clara Adams to the great meeting of the club when you are to wind up the year with such a flourish?" that her conscience began to prick her.

"Nobody has asked her," she answered, "and she is dying to come. She isn't coming back to school next year, you know."

"Yes, I think you told me that. I feel very sorry for her. Of course, she is not at all the kind of child I should choose for a companion for my little girl, but I am very glad you have tried to be kind to her, though I cannot say I regret her leaving the school you attend."

Edna was silent for a moment and so was her mother who presently asked: "Have you given out all your invitations, dear?"

"No, mother, I still have one."

"Whom did you send the other to?"

"Miss Martin. She and her father were so nice to me at the fair you know, but one of the other girls has invited Mr. Martin."

"I see. That was certainly a very good choice for you to make."

85

"I can't quite decide about the other one," Edna went on. "I want to give it to the one who wants it most, of the two girls at school who would love to have it."

"Is one of them Clara Adams?"

"Oh, mother, no. Nobody wants her." Then after a silence, "I suppose she wants to come badder than anyone else, but—mother, do you think, do you really think I ought to invite her?"

"Why, my dear, that is for you to decide."

"Oh, dear," Edna gave a long sigh. Never in her life had she been more put to it to make up her mind. "I don't want to one bit," she declared after a moment's thought. "All of the girls will be down on me and say I am a silly goose and all that."

"It is probably your very last chance of doing her a kindness as she will possibly not cross your path again," Mrs. Conway reminded her.

Edna drew a longer sigh than before. The situation was getting harder and harder. "Mother," she said with a woebegone face, "why do the rightest things always be the hardest ones?"

"I don't think they always are, dear child. Is this so very hard?"

"Oh, yes. I think it is the hardest thing I most ever had to do. Even last year when those things about Louis worried me so, I didn't mind so much, for I was really fond of Louis. He was my cousin and it seemed more as if I ought to."

"Well, dearie, suppose you think over it a while. You can keep back your invitation till the very last minute, you know, for if you do decide to let Clara have it, she will be glad to accept even at the eleventh hour, I am sure."

"Suppose she should say horrid mean things and stir up a fuss as she does so many times, I should feel so badly."

"I don't believe she would do that because she would be enjoying herself and would probably be on her best behavior. If you like, I will see that she sits next to me which would be quite right if she should be your guest, and it will not spoil my pleasure if she should make disagreeable remarks."

Edna went over and leaned her elbows on her mother's lap, looking up in her face and asking. "What would you say to yourself if she made disagreeable remarks?"

"I should say, 'Never mind; I am so happy that my own darling little girl made the sacrifice of asking her that nothing else matters much.'"

"And you wouldn't say anything to her?"

"I should, no doubt, say several things to her," replied Mrs. Conway kissing the eager face uplifted toward hers.

Edna went over to the window and stood there a long time, but she saw none of the things she looked out upon. She was having a sharp struggle. Clara and her mother against all the girls in the club, that was the way it seemed to be, but finally the former conquered and she went back to where her mother still sat. "Mother," she said firmly, "I am going to invite Clara. I have made up my mind. Will you please ask Agnes and Celia to take my part?"

"My blessed child, of course I will. What sort of a Golden Rule would it be that allowed a little girl to be chidden for carrying out its precepts. As president of your club, Agnes will surely see that you are acting upon its principles, and Celia, too, must see it. They must not let their enjoyment and their love of harmony make them forget that part."

Then Edna snuggled very close to her mother and felt comforted. "I am not going to keep her from knowing," she said. "I'll tell her first thing, so she can have the fun of looking forward to it." When Edna did a thing there was no doing it by halves.

Therefore it was a surprised and delighted Clara who received her invitation the next day, and to Edna's great satisfaction all the good in the girl rose to the occasion. "I think you are the very sweetest girl I ever knew, Edna Conway," she said, "and I am sorry, I really am, that I haven't always been friends with you. I was horrid, often I was," and this was Edna's compensation.

Such a flutter and flurry and whispering and giggling there was on that afternoon when everything was in readiness for the little flower play. There was quite a large audience gathered on the smooth green lawn where seats had been placed for them. The shrubs and flower beds with trees beyond made a fine background for the stretch of terrace, which became a stage for the occasion. Jennie in a fuzzy grayish brown frock with a hood, made a dear little Pussy Willow, Edna in pink with her rosy cheeks was the very picture of Pinky Blooms, Dorothy's golden head made a lovely centre for Daisy White, while as for Ben, the big giant, he was the roughest, toughest old Pine Knot one could imagine.

"If only Miss Eloise could be here to see us," said Edna as she peeped from behind the leafy screen which hid the flower fairies from view.

Dorothy was peeping, too, and presently she exclaimed, "She is here! Oh, Edna, she is here! See, they are bringing her now!" And sure enough, there in her wheeled chair was Miss Eloise, her lovely face all smiles as her sister and Mr. Ramsey pushed her chair along.

87

"I do believe Mrs. Ramsey brought her out," cried Edna.

"She did," Jennie told them, "I didn't tell, because I thought it would be such a nice surprise for everybody."

A surprise it was indeed, and because of her presence, or because it is generally so, they all did much better than at any of their rehearsals and received such applause as quite overpowered them. Then Mr. Ramsey raised a call for "Author! Author!" So after some little delay Ben, still in his giant's dress, was brought around and wheeled Miss Eloise out to the very front where she was given another round of applause and more flowers than she could hold. She quite forgot herself in her anxiety that Ben should receive what was due to him and all unmindful of the large audience, she cried out, "Oh, but I did so little; it is all Ben's plan!"

Then Ben was cheered, and in the midst of such very special demonstrations he beat a retreat.

Clara established by Mrs. Conway's side had not a word of anything but praise and delight, and after the little players came out to mix with their friends she sought out Edna. "It was the loveliest thing I ever saw," she told her, "and I do thank you for letting me come."

"She was really very decent," said the girls, looking after her as she started for home with her mother who called for her.

Edna watched her out of sight, a feeling of pity mingled with gladness in her heart. And so Clara Adams passed out of her life, for before another year the entire family had moved out west, and the places which saw Clara Adams saw her no more.

The stars were coming out before they all left Mrs. MacDonald's. The guests had taken their departure earlier and had been as complimentary as anyone could desire. Miss Eloise, tired but very happy, had gone off with the Ramseys in their motor-car. Edna, Dorothy and Margaret walked down to the gate to watch the sunset, all yellow and glowing.

"Miss Newman looked almost pretty," said Dorothy. "She had such a dear frock on and her hair is much nicer the way she wore it to-day. I shall feel so very different about having her for a teacher next year."

"So shall I," agreed Edna.

Moggins, Margaret's cat had sought them out and was rubbing up against his little mistress. "Oh, you poor dear, I don't believe anyone has thought to give you your milk," said Margaret. So she went off with the cat in her arms.

Then "Where are you, Dorothy?" cried her sister, and Dorothy scampered off that she might not be left behind on the homeward walk.

Edna walked slowly toward the house. Halfway up the walk she met Uncle Justus. "I was just coming for you to walk home with me," he told her. "Your aunt and I are going to stay all night."

"I'm glad of that," Edna replied slipping her hand into his.

They walked on toward the road, quite silent for a few moments, till Edna looking up, said, "Uncle Justus, I think you have a perfectly lovely school."

He smiled down at her.

"I have some perfectly lovely pupils," he answered with a smile.

THE END

Ingram Content Group UK Ltd.
Milton Keynes UK
UKHW040735210723
425555UK00004B/215

9 791041 818471